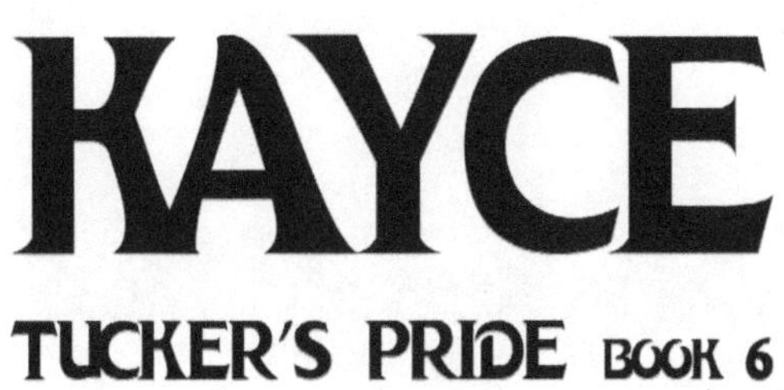

KAYCE

TUCKER'S PRIDE BOOK 6

KATHI S. BARTON

This is a work of fiction. Names, characters, places, and incidents are products of the author's imagination or are used fictitiously and are not to be construed as real. Any resemblance to actual events, locations, organizations, or persons, living or dead, is entirely coincidental.

World Castle Publishing, LLC
Pensacola, Florida

Hardback ISBN: 9798248375615
Paperback ISBN: 9798891265226
eBook ISBN: 9798891265233
First Edition World Castle Publishing, LLC, April 6, 2026
http://www.worldcastlepublishing.com
Licensing Notes

Cover: Cover Designs by Karen
Editor: Karen Fuller

Chapter 1

Kayce only had three more weeks to go, and he'd be able to leave the firm he'd been a part of. Having his name on the outside wall was great, but he'd never hated to work at a place like he did this one. The other doctors were selfish and mean. They wanted nothing to do with one another outside the offices, and they didn't have each other's backs. Ever. The nurses weren't that much better in that they stuck together and didn't help out when there was a problem. He wasn't going to take his nurse with him when he left. He was going to let her be with the other bastards that were there.

He had a place all picked out where he was going to hold his practice. Being a pediatrician was all he had ever wanted to be when he'd been growing up. Now that he was going to be out on his own, he was excited for the next chapter of his life to begin and put the other place as far behind him as he could. He'd made no friends, and he didn't feel bad about giving his notice when they were all scrambling to find someone to replace him.

"Doctor Tucker, you have a call on line two. I believe it's your brother Hudson. He sounds like him anyway." He went to his office to take the call, wondering why he'd not reached out to him. As soon as he put the receiver to his ear, he felt his lion wrap around him tightly.

"Hud fell down the stairs. I'm trying not to freak out here, but should there be that much blood?" He asked him if anything was broken. "His leg is for sure. I can see the bone sticking up from his leg. But there's so much blood. I'm worried that he might have cut a vein or something."

"Stop looking for trouble. Did you call an ambulance?" He said that he had first thing. "All right. I'm nearly done here. I'll meet the two of you there. Don't be surprised if they take him right away for x-rays. I'm going to call in orders on my way in."

"Thanks. I told them that it wasn't a good idea to go sliding down the stairs. Remember when we used to do that? I think you fell and broke something, too." He said he'd broken his wrist. "That's right. I remember now. The ambulance is here now, so I'm going to go with them. The neighborhood teenager is coming over to watch the other two for me while I'm gone. I've called Ivy as well."

"Good. Then I'll see you there." Getting out of his last patient wasn't all that difficult. Since she never showed up on time, and he'd told her the last time that if she wasn't there on time, he wasn't going to see her, he just left. Being forty-five minutes late would mess up his entire day when she was supposed to be there before noon.

Driving to the hospital, he called in orders for his nephew. This was the second time that Hud had been hurt at home, and he was going to have to have words with the little boy if he didn't stop taking so many chances. He couldn't really blame him; he'd been a risk taker too when he'd been his age and had gotten himself in all kinds of bad situations. He was going to have to explain that getting hurt had consequences.

His leg was indeed broken and needed to have surgery on it. While he could assist when something like this came up, he left that kind of thing to the professionals, like surgeons who dealt with broken bones every day. He spoke to Ivy and Hudson to tell them what was going on, and didn't have to tell them that he'd been lucky that he'd been at home when it had happened. Doing things like he'd been doing might have broken his fool neck had he slipped off the staircase a little further up than he had and landed on his head. His parents had already done that before they got to the hospital. He was glad. It saved him from having to be the bad uncle who yelled at him.

After surgery, Hud was put into his room to recuperate. He'd told his parents not to allow him to shift for a couple of weeks so that he'd learn his lesson. Ivy was all for it, but Hudson was more than a little bit cautious. He'd said that boys will be boys and that he'd done the same thing as a child. He thought that after a couple of weeks of going through the pain of the break, he might learn something, but he was only the doctor uncle and not the parent.

Going home that night after talking to Hud, he realized that he only had about four days left on his term with the doctors park he was working with, if he didn't count his days off or the weekends. That made him feel so much better, so when his phone rang, he was glad to have someone calling him other than the hospital.

"She's been hurt bad, doc. I need for you to come out and see to her." He asked who it was. "It's me, William Toby, senior. Molly, my granddaughter, has been beaten up, and she's in a bad way. Can you come out and convince her she needs to go to the hospital? She's in a bad way, she is."

"I'll be out. Call an ambulance anyway if you think she needs it, and I'll be there when they get there." He said that he'd do that, but she'd be powerful mad. "Is she at least conscious? That would help me in dealing with her when I get there."

"She's in and out of it. My son…damn him. If he were here, I'd knock the shit right out of him. He's done this to her, and there ain't nobody going to tell me different." Grabbing his coat, he was out the door while still talking to William. "He thinks it's funny to have her around where he can beat her senseless. Poor baby. She's only home for another day or two and has to go back. I don't think she's going to make it. Going back, I mean. Lord, I hope she don't die. She's all the family that I have left that I claim."

"I'm on my way, Mr. William. I'll be there soon." He didn't rush; there was no point in his getting into an accident, too. However, he did pause at a couple of lights instead of stopping at them. As soon as he pulled in, the ambulance pulled in right behind him. he thought that he'd done good to beat the medics. "All right. Let's see what we have here."

It took him twenty minutes to figure out all her wounds. She'd been beaten pretty good with someone's fists, and he wanted to find the man responsible and teach him a few lessons as well. When she looked up at him, he asked her if she'd gotten in a few punches of her own. Laughing, then stopping when he assumed that it hurt too bad, she said he was more than likely in the emergency department now. She'd gotten him good.

"Good for you. But I'm afraid that you're going to have to go into the hospital too for some x-rays. And a few other tests. Did he hit you with anything other than his fists?" She said that he'd had a knife, but she'd been able to take that from him. "Good for you. All right, I'm going to have the medics give you something for the pain that I'm sure you're in, so that traveling will be a bit easier on you." He moved out of the way so that they could do what they came here for.

"I have to call my boss." He said that they'd get her a phone when they had more answers. "He's going to be pissed off, but I can handle him. He might think that he's all that, but he's just a wussy in his heart. He is kinda sweet on me." That made his lion want to do the other man harm, but he didn't do anything more than wait until she was in the ambulance. "You'll have to fill out some paperwork if I'm going to be hanging around much longer. I have a duty to my country that I can shirk on now. I only have a few more months to go."

"What are you in the service for?" She told him that it was to get away from her family. "As good a reason as any, I would imagine. Let the drugs take you under, and we can get you loaded up in the ambulance. That way, we can get you taken care of when you get to the hospital."

"Look out for my dad. He's not going to be in a good mood after what I did to him. He might just have you for breakfast." He said that he could hold his own. "I'm sure you can, but he fights dirty and doesn't care who gets hurt while he's making a name for himself. Mostly being an idiot, but I think you understand, having spent some time with him when Pop-pop was staying at the hospital."

"He didn't strike me as a man who had all his marbles." She laughed and started falling asleep. "Let the drugs take you under, Molly. You might feel better when you wake up."

Nodding, she told him that she was going to be fine and he believed her. She had something about her that made him want to pick her up into his arms and hold her until she was better. However, he knew that she'd kick his ass if he were to try that.

She didn't have any broken bones, and he was surprised by that. He'd thought for sure that she had at least three ribs broken when she'd been at the house. Now all she had was some deep bruising and some contusions as well. He had stitches put in her arms where she'd been cut with the knife, and was happy that she was doing so well. Mr. William seemed to be happy with the results, and that was more than he could have hoped for. He liked the elderly man and hated to see him so worried about his granddaughter.

After admitting her for her concussion, he decided to check on a couple of his patients. One had had their tonsils taken out this morning, and he released her so that she could be pampered at home. The other was his nephew, and since he was also doing fine, he decided that he'd release him in the morning. He would get more than enough care at home, and he wasn't worried about him not getting the care that he needed. Kayce was only a phone call away and knew that Hudson or Ivy would call him if anything came up.

On his way home, he picked up something to

eat. It had been a long day, and he was exhausted. It wasn't until he'd had his shower and eaten that he went up to bed. Soon he'd be able to shift, and he couldn't wait until all the aches and pains of helping out at the hospital were gone.

He'd been in the emergency department when a man came in who had been high on something. He had been able to get a gun into the place and had planned to kill himself and whoever tried to stop him. Since he was the only shifter on site, he wrestled the gun away from the man but sustained quite a few injuries himself in the process. Broken ribs and a bloodied nose were only a few of the injuries that he'd gotten when the man tried to kill him. Lucky for him, he'd not been shot in the process, but it was for the good, he kept telling himself, and that was all that mattered. No one else was hurt, for which he was grateful.

After waking up the next morning, he was happy to feel better. The ache in his shoulders was still there, but it wasn't nearly as bad as it had been a week ago when he'd been hurt. Even his mouth felt better than it had previously. Getting ready for work, he was glad that he wasn't on call anymore until the end of his time with the group he was in. He couldn't wait to get out of the place and hang his own shingle out where he could pick and choose his own patients.

The day started off all right. Of course, the doctors didn't talk much to him. He was fine with that as he didn't care for them in the first place. As soon as lunch rolled around, he'd seen three patients, and most of it was minor stuff. One of them had to have a physical for the upcoming sports season, and he was happy to tell the young man that he passed. He remembered playing football in high school and sort of was jealous of the boy to be able to play something that he obviously loved. After lunch, it wasn't much different. After two, when his last patient was gone, he made his way to the hospital to check on Molly and Hud, his nephew.

Both were doing well, and he got to see Mr. William when he was there visiting his granddaughter. She wasn't in a good mood, having talked to her boss, he was told, but he was glad to be able to release her as well. Once he signed off on the paperwork, he was free for the rest of the evening. He could use it as he was still trying to catch up on sleep that he'd missed for the last few days.

As soon as he was home, he crashed on the couch and went to sleep. It didn't matter to him that he had a nice, comfy bed to sleep in. He was just too tired to go up and get into his tonight. As soon as his head hit the pillow, he closed his eyes. After tomorrow, he only had two more days, and he couldn't wait. He was going to take a month off just to relax and chill out until he found himself a building that he could work in. It might take him that long as there were very little empty buildings around town nowadays, and he was happy for that as well.

Getting up once to go to the bathroom, he had no trouble at all making his way there and back to the couch. He'd been sleeping so hard that his shoulder was a little stiff, but other than that, he was doing fine. Still sleeping on the couch had better appeal for him than going up to his bedroom and going to sleep again. He was just too tired and didn't care if he had to sleep on the floor, so long as he didn't have to go up any stairs to get there.

~*~

Molly was feeling better than she had in the last couple of days. Her pop-pop was pampering her a bit too much, but she loved him and could forgive him most anything. As soon as he was out of the room, getting her a cup of coffee, she sat up higher on the couch and looked around the vast room.

This room had always been her favorite. When she was just a child and staying with her pop-pop and Grannie, they had the best times watching television and eating popcorn. Of course, back then they'd had staff. Pop-pop had told her once that he'd outgrown having someone wait on him, and that was why he'd let them go. She thought it had more to do with him having very little money, but she never said that to him. Things were tight around the house, and she knew it by helping him pay his bills every month. It didn't help that her two brothers, Seth and Ryan, were forever trying to take Pop-pop's social security check along with her dad.

She thought it would have been better for them if they just got a job, but she didn't tell them that. The one time she'd suggested it, she'd been barely sixteen and had nearly died from the beating that they'd given her. All three of them had taken turns knocking her around until she had to spend a week in the hospital. Never again did she suggest they do anything. But she was trained now in how to defend herself and never passed up an opportunity to show them how much training she'd had.

"I was just having a look at my leg. I'm telling you that it's nearly healed up, and the bruising isn't as bad as it was either. That doc must have used some of his mojo on me and got me to feeling better, too. I feel like I could take on William Toby and come out on top." He laughed. "I won't, mind you, but I was just thinking about how much better I'm feeling. Did you know that the doc is a lion? He's about the nicest shifter I ever known."

"How many shifters do you know, Pop-pop?" He said that he'd been around them all his life and never had a problem with a single one of them. "I know a couple, too. Most of them are nice, but every once in a while, you run into a bad apple. They are usually mean to everyone, so I don't give them much mind. How about for dinner we have us a pizza? I'll pay for it. Dad didn't get all my money the other day, only what I wanted him to have."

She stretched her jaw and felt it pop. It was feeling better, too, after the beating that she took from her dad. She could eat now and wasn't above slicing her pizza with a knife and fork just so she didn't have to eat any more leftovers. The women around town had been bringing Pop-pop food every week since her grandmother had passed away, and she wanted some real food. Pizza was about as real as it got for her nowadays.

Molly had gotten an extra week off when she'd called her boss. She'd been set to go back out of the country as soon as she visited her grandda, but it had been hard to do much of anything after she'd gotten beaten up. He wasn't happy that she had been hurt, but he knew about her family more than anyone else did, and she figured that if anyone understood her getting knocked around, it would have been him. Her father was a prick.

Seth and Ryan weren't nearly as bad as their dad, but they would be egged on by him when things needed to be taken too far. Seth was the youngest and by far the stupidest of the three of them. She'd thought that he'd had some mental issues, but the doctor said he was smart for his age, just mean. She believed it. He was as mean as their dad when it suited him.

Ryan would stand back and watch what the other two were doing before he joined in. Ryan, unlike Seth, had spent some time in prison and swore he'd never go back. She figured that he'd learned something about being behind bars, but she couldn't figure out what that might be. He would kill her if given the chance, and that was why she never gave them the opportunity to do much more than knock her around until this last time.

They'd caught her off her guard. While in the kitchen making grilled cheese for her and her grandda, something had hit her from behind and she'd been knocked out. It wasn't until the pain she was in woke her up that she knew that she'd been beaten badly. It still surprised her that she didn't have any broken bones. They'd kicked her while she was down, and she would swear that some of her ribs had been broken while out.

"I'd love to have some pizza. Some of that hot sauce on it that we like too." Molly told him that they had the hot sauce in the cabinet and would get it out when it arrived. "I'll call and order it for us, and you can pay. I'd do it, honey, but I'm on a tight budget as you know."

"I know. I understand what it's like to be on a budget." He ordered them a large pie that they'd share with onions and mushrooms on it. The hot sauce that they'd enjoy on it was nothing more than hot wing sauce, but it was better than just a plain old pizza, and they'd both have a good meal. As soon as it came, she got up to get the sauce while he was clearing a place at the table for them to eat.

"I feel like I'm about healed up, too. It's amazing. I've never felt like this after a good beating from them." Pop-pop told her that he wished he could have done more, but he'd been afraid of them hurting him, too. "You did the right thing in hiding from them. Don't ever put yourself in a position where you are going to be hurt by them for me. I should have known that they'd be around. They just caught me off guard there, and it won't happen again. Not so long as I can get the jump on them."

"It scared me a bit when you could barely breathe. And all that blood, too. I never seen the likes of it." She watched as he shivered and put his slice back on the box. "I tell you something, baby girl. I'm thinking that I'm getting too old to have them coming here and beating on me. I've been thinking of giving you this house and moving into a nursing home. I've even been looking at the best ones."

"We don't need to talk about that now, do we?" He nodded and told her that he'd given it a great deal of thought and wanted her to take him to the one he'd been looking at. "I don't want you to do that, but if you have your heart set on it, I'll take you there in the morning. I sure will miss coming here to be with you."

"That's the thing about this place I've been looking into. It has two bedrooms for those who want them, and you could stay with me for a while when you come home. You don't have that much longer to go, do you?" She told him how many days she had left to be in the service. "No time at all when you think about how long you've been in it. I tell you, it was the best advice I could have given you when you turned eighteen and joined the service. You've been able to help me when I needed it, and I've loved all the stories that you've told me. Those are stories that I'm going to take to my Sally when I go. She'll be tickled pink that I have so much to tell her."

"She will at that." She thought about the nursing home and knew that if he'd done any research on it, she'd be happy with what he was doing. "I'll take you there tomorrow. How much more than your check is it going to cost you? You know that I'll help you when you need it."

"Nothing much more than what I'm paying now. Without having to pay for the utilities and such, I'd be coming out ahead. Not to mention I'd be getting three meals a day that I don't have to mess with. I like that part best of all. And having a nice room for you to stay in when you come to visit me. The best part is that I'll be safe from my son and grandsons. They won't be able to get into the place without me telling them that it's all right. I decided that the only person that I'm going to allow to visit me is you." He took her hand into his much larger one and patted it. "I love you, Molly, my dear. I miss you so much when you're gone."

"I love you, Pop-pop." He wiped his napkin over his face and told her that he loved her more. "We'll head over there in the morning to get you signed in. With dad in the hospital still, we'll be able to get you there without him knowing. I think that's going to be our best bet in keeping you safe."

"This will work out better, you'll see." He finished up his half of the pizza and took one of her slices. She wasn't as hungry as he'd been, apparently, and she was glad that he had such a good appetite. He wasn't a big man, but tall. Since he'd always eaten so well, she never worried about him having any trouble with being too thin. She loved the old man and would move heaven and earth for him if there was something that he needed.

The next morning, after pancakes for breakfast that she'd made them, he was ready to go. He'd even been packed to stay when they got the paperwork finished. He'd really put a lot of thought into this, and she was happy that he was going to be safe. Now, if she could figure out a way to make herself safe, she'd feel so much better. But she was leaving in a few days and would be about as far from them as she could get. They wouldn't know how to get in touch with her either.

The place had charm, she'd give it that. As soon as the paperwork had been filled out and filed, he was set to be living there. As he pulled out his luggage from her rental, she felt like he was running away from home and told him as much.

"I sort of feel like that. Like I'm on some new adventure too." He laughed, and she had to smile. "This will be one more thing that I can do for myself before I'm kicking up roses. You'll come here to visit me, won't you, little bit?"

"Nothing could keep me away." He nodded as they set up his room. he wasn't allowed to cook in his room, for which she was grateful, and he could have a coffee pot so long as he didn't leave it on all the time. He only drank one cup a day and rarely, if ever, had more than that. She was just putting the last of his clothing away when he turned to her. "What is it? Have you changed your mind already?"

"The house is in your name. It has been since you were home the last time." She said that he didn't have to do that. "I do. It belongs to you. Please tell me that you're going to find you a nice young man and bring the house to life again."

"I'll look, but the chances aren't all that good that someone is going to take me on with my family around." He told her that he'd feel better about things if she were to at least try. "I'll try. I don't want anything to do with the men that I see every day. Perhaps when I get out, I'll find me a nice young man and have twenty babies. How about that?"

"So long as you're happy and safe, I don't care if you have fifty children." They both laughed, and she hugged him. "Now, let's go see what they have to offer for lunch. That was nice of the woman who signed me in to tell us that you could join me for lunch. I think that my first meal here should be with the one person that I love more than I do myself."

The lunch was better than she thought it would be. It was stroganoff and homemade noodles. She had a bit of sour cream on hers, and he sopped up his gravy with her slices of bread. She thought her grandda looked better than he had in the last few days, and she thought that he'd figured that she'd not be all right with him moving into the nursing home. It was more like an assisted living, but she was fine with it. Telling him that she felt better about him being someplace where someone was going to be watching over him made them both feel good. As soon as she was ready to leave, they both got teary-eyed.

"I'm going to miss you tonight." He said that he'd call her later. "You'd better. I can't go to sleep without you telling me goodnight."

"I know the feeling." He didn't tell her goodbye like he would have if she were leaving him. Instead, he told her that he'd see her later. On the way home, she bawled her eyes out, missing him already, but she knew in her heart that this was for the best, no matter how much she didn't like being in the big house all on her own.

The house seemed so empty to her now. Since she wanted to stay there until she had to leave, she ran the vacuum and did the few dishes from this morning. By the time she was finished dusting, Molly figured that she'd cried about a bucket of tears and was missing her grandda more than she thought possible. She kept telling herself that he was safe and that's all that mattered.

Chapter 2

Kayce slept until seven, well past when he normally got up. As he was going through his morning list of things that he had to do, he kept thinking about Molly Toby and her grandda. He didn't know why they'd been on his mind, but he couldn't shake the feelings that he needed to do something for them.

He'd seen William Junior in the hospital. He'd been in worse shape than his daughter had been, and he was happy that she'd been able to stand up for herself. He'd had a total of four broken ribs as well as about fifty stitches on his body, which made him think that he'd not want to mess with Molly when she was in that kind of mood. He remembered that she'd been beaten up too, but he was happy that she was on the mend and staying with her grandda while he was recuperating too. When his phone rang, he couldn't believe that it was Mr. William calling him.

"I moved out of the big house and have moved into some assisted living." He never started a conversation with hello or hi. Just launched into the conversation like they'd been talking all along. "Molly is at the big house all on her own. I just wanted to let you know in the event that you come looking for me.

She's going back in the service tomorrow and will be gone for a few weeks before her vacation starts again. She's using up all the time that she'd built up so that she doesn't lose it when she gets out."

"How is she feeling? And I'm happy that you've gotten someone to take over your care. You might have stayed there before now, and you wouldn't have fallen. But I'm happy for you."

"I am too. They've been nice as can be to me since I got here yesterday. I have my own rooms and one for Molly when she comes to visit." He told him some of the rules that he had to follow and found them to be just what the elderly man needed. Not to cook in his rooms was a big one that people his age struggled with. "I've ordered myself a television for me to watch when my shows come on. Molly and I loved to watch them game shows when they come on in the evening. I have to tell you, other than missing my girl, I slept well last night. Didn't think that I would with the boys out there hunting me down."

"The brothers are in jail for assault. Your son is in the hospital still and will serve his time when he gets out. I didn't know that Molly had pressed charges against them. It's the best way to go." He said that she was a smart girl. "I would say so. And she did a number on her father, too. He's going to be hurting for a while yet."

Sometimes, like now, he would think of Molly's

injuries and wonder why he'd been so wrong about her having broken bones. He knew that on some level, he wasn't right all the time, but he'd been so sure when he'd seen her that she had at least three broken ribs and her wrist broken. The fact that he'd been able to release her made him think that he needed to be more careful in the future.

"I've never been so ashamed of anyone in my entire life than I am of them boys. To think that instead of getting a job, they think it's easier to beat an old man up for his only income just boggles my mind." He told him he was sorry. "So am I. I wished my wife were still around. She'd surely have them put away. I made a promise to Molly that when they come around to beat me up, I'm going to press charges against them. Not that I think they'll be able to get me while I'm in here, but I'm going to be more careful about that, too. You can bank on that."

"Good. I know a few people like your family, and I wouldn't trust them as far as I could toss them." He laughed, and it made Kayce smile. "If you ever need anything from me, Mr. William, you give me a call. I'll be there as fast as I can. I see a couple of people at that assisted living place, and if you don't mind, I'll stop by to see you sometimes."

"I'd like that. Yes, sir. I'd like that very much." They rang off, and he put his phone away. For some reason, he didn't feel like the connection had been enough and decided to go and check on Molly. What harm could it do, he asked himself. She was his patient, and he could check on her when she needed it.

On the way to the house, he thought about the big mammoth of a building. He knew from talking to Mr. William that the place had eight bedrooms. He also told him that it would need some work to get it back in shape, but it was just the kind of house he'd been looking for when he'd been house hunting. Big enough to spread out in and with the outbuildings around the place, he could easily set himself up an office where he could do some doctoring in. Just as he pulled into the driveway, he had a sudden thought. Could Molly be his mate?

Things about her started falling into place. She'd healed faster than he'd thought. Even though he'd been to see her when she'd been beaten, she'd healed with him there. As he was ticking off the list of things that made sense to him, he realized that she might well be his mate. While sitting in his car thinking about the other things that were going on, he changed his clothing into something more comfortable and knew without a doubt that she was the one. Getting out of his car, he was smiling when he went to the door.

"I just ordered dinner, and I thought you were him." He said that he'd come by to check on her and was pleased that she was getting around so well. "I've been feeling pretty good for the last two days. But I got a craving for some Chinese food and ordered enough that I could take leftovers into my pop-pop for his lunch tomorrow. You might as well join me."

She didn't sound thrilled about him joining her, and that made him laugh. When he inhaled deeply when her back was turned to him, he smiled at that, too. She called to him; her scent did, and he couldn't have been more happy. As he was closing the door, another car pulled into the driveway, and he saw it was the delivery person. Perfect timing. He might well call in a second order if she didn't order enough for the two of them. He was suddenly hungry, too.

She had ordered a great deal, and he was happy about that. Offering to pay for his half, she said that he could get it the next time she was in town. Kayce asked when she was leaving, and his heart did a little jump. Tomorrow night. That didn't leave them much time to get to know one another, and that sort of depressed him.

"What do you know about shifters?" She bit into her egg roll and told him that she'd already figured it out. "Figured out what? That I belong to you?"

"Mates. The two of us are. You're the only stranger that I've seen in the past few days, and I know that I shouldn't have been healed already. Do you want some soup? I got a lot of it because Pop-pop loves it when it's hot." He told her that he'd love some but would put in another order so she could take some to her grandda. "All right. I'm going to miss this when I'm overseas, but I only have a few months left to go. Most of it will be eaten up in time off. I have a lot of it built up."

She handed him a menu, and he ordered enough that he could take some to work for himself tomorrow. He loved egg rolls, and these seemed to hit the spot. While they were waiting for the second order, she asked him what he was going to do without her being around all the time.

"I don't know. I don't feel the need to mark you or anything. I do want to protect you from your family, but I think that you'd do a better job than I would." She told him that she'd been trained in hand to hand combat. "I figured as much. It's like I know that you're going to be leaving soon, but I'm all right with that. So long as you come back to me when your time is up."

"I don't know what to think about my being your mate." He corrected her. "Whatever. Who cares who belongs to who? We're mates, and that's all that matters. I do have a few rules about stuff. I won't quit what I'm doing. I can get all my benefits if I hang out for the rest of my enlistment, and I don't want to lose that."

"I understand that completely." He told her how he'd been wanting out of the doctors' group that he's been in and stuck it out so that he'd not have to pay for it. "I only have tomorrow to go, and then I'll be finished with them. Would you like to live here when you get out? It's a charming house if a little bit out of date."

"It's a lot out of date, but I would love to live here. There are things that it needs that I can afford, but I was waiting until I had the money to pay for them. The roof, for example. It needs to be replaced like last year." He asked about the kitchen. "It's a couple of centuries out of date, but it had good walls, my grannie used to say. It will take a lot to get it back up to this century."

"I have the money that we can start on it as soon as your grandfather gives us permission." She said that as of last year, she owned the house. "Good. We can get started on it right away. While you're gone, I can oversee what's going on and keep you up to date on the changes."

"This is all moving fast, don't you think? I mean, I only just figured out that we're mates yesterday." He said that he'd figured it out when he pulled into her driveway. "A little slow, aren't you? I mean, aren't you guys like right on top of marking your mates so that everyone knows that I belong to you?"

"I feel no need to mark you as you said. I just feel good that you're here for me and that we seem to be able to get along." She ate the last of the egg rolls when the doorbell rang again. "That'll be the rest of the food. I hope that it's enough. I've never been this hungry in a while. It feels good."

They finished all but about a quart of the soup and two egg rolls. She was happy with that as it would be perfect for her grandda. Cleaning up the mess they'd made in the dining room, he got to see the kitchen and wasn't surprised that she'd been right. It did need a great deal of work. He would start on it tomorrow if she'd let him.

They talked about the things that needed to be done to the house, and he made notes. He'd, like his family had always been a note taker and now was no different. As they toured the house, looking at all the bedrooms too, he was amazed that someone hadn't done anything to it before now. But then she explained that her grandda had been on a limited budget and didn't have it to make sure that it was in working order.

"The kitchen is going to be the most expensive to bring up to code or even date. It needs to have the walls redone as well as all new appliances. With that, there will probably need to be some wiring done so that nothing catches on fire while we renovate." He said that he knew that the foundation had its own construction team that he could maybe use, and thought they'd do a good job. "Plus, it will need the bathrooms redone. There are six of them in the house, plus three half baths."

"Has it been in your family for very long?" She said that her grandfather had been born in the house, and it had been added onto over the years. "I'm excited about getting started. What do you say we start on it tomorrow after you're gone and I can make sure that things are done the way that we want?"

"I'd like that. But keep track of all the money you put into it. I have a bonus check coming for mustering out of the service that will be nice to add to it. Plus, I've never really spent all that much money when I was overseas, so I've managed to save a great deal that way." He told her that he'd been able to save too, and he had accumulated a great deal of money just by investing in things that he found interesting. "Good. The land around the house is worth some money, and we can borrow against that should we need more money. The house has been paid off for a decade or two, and all the taxes have been paid yearly. I made sure of that for my grandda."

She had an idea about what she wanted in the kitchen. He wanted a large enough space that they could eat in it if they wished. Of course, with them both working, they'd need staff, but that wasn't something they had to do right now. He did ask her about the outbuildings and whether or not he could use one of them for his practice.

"One of them was an office of sorts before I left for the service. You should have a look at them in the morning before I leave. We should also go to the bank so that we can have your name on the deed, so that there won't be any trouble with you doing the renovations. I'd hate for you to get started only to have to stop almost as soon as the first nail was taken out of the walls." They still had time tonight, and that's where they headed. And just like that, he had a house in his name and a mate all in one setting. "I feel like I'm settled. Like with you right here, I can function like I've never been able to before."

"I feel the same way. Like you've taken a burden off my shoulders that I didn't know was there. I feel good about what we've accomplished so far." She nodded as they drove to the bank. With the deed in hand, she was ready to do what was necessary, and so was he. This was the strangest mate finding that he'd ever heard of. In less than twenty-four hours, she'd be gone, and he'd be redoing their home. He wondered what his family would say if they knew right now.

~*~

Molly gathered her gear and made her way to the registration office. She was to fly out in the morning on a transport plane and wasn't looking forward to returning. Everything had started to come together just as she was leaving, and she didn't want to leave behind the two people who had made it happen. Pop-pop and Kayce.

Pop-pop was in good hands. The nursing home/ assisted living place was top-rated, and she liked that he had his own rooms. There were other things that he could take advantage of as well. There was an in-house doctor that he could go see. A barber, someone to take care of his feet when he needed. And best of all, that she could see, was that he'd be safe, as they had a system installed where only certain people on a list could come in and see the guests there. Her pop-pop had put not just her on the list, but Kayce, too, as his doctor friend.

"Sergeant Toby, you have a note here with your name on it. See that you read it before you leave." She said that she would and was handed an official-looking envelope with her name typed across the front. Also on it was written the word 'Urgent'. "That came in about an hour ago, and I'm to wait for an answer."

"Yes, sir." Going to the little row of chairs, she put her stuff down in favor of opening the envelope. It was just one sheet of paper, and it was typewritten. Opening up the message, she had to frown. It was from her boss. "It says here that I'm to report for duty at the White House ASAP. Do you know what sort of answer I was supposed to give you? This just says report, no question."

"I would imagine that it's making sure you're going to report." Why the hell wouldn't she? I mean, it wasn't like it was an invitation to a ball or something. "Are you going to report to the W. H.?"

"Of course I am. Sir." She nearly forgot where she was for a moment and had to retrain herself in speaking to others. She was already in Washington after a long flight and was ready for some downtime. But she was going to have to make her way to the White House now for god only knew what reason. "Is there a transport going there?"

"A limo will pick you up. Don't get used to this kind of treatment all the time. But I was to send for one to pick you up and then later take you back here. Do you have everything you need?" How the hell would she know, but she answered yes, sir, to the man in uniform so that she could get on her way. "It will arrive within the hour, so be ready."

Good, she thought to herself, a whole hour to wonder why she was headed to the White House to see her boss. The boss of all bosses, as it turned out. The President of the United States. Sitting down in one of the many chairs in the big office, she watched the front doors. Who knew when the limo was going to come and get her and why? As far as she was concerned, she'd done nothing wrong while in the service but do her job to the best of her abilities.

"Hello?" She looked around for someone speaking to her and found that she was all alone in the room. *"I'll be there in a jiffy."*

A woman appeared sitting next to her, and she looked around to see if anyone else could see her. Leaning back in her chair, she asked the woman who she was and how she got here.

"I'm Parker, grand witch of all witches. Please tell me that you believe in witches. There are a lot of us around. None like me, I'm happy to say, but there are plenty of lesser witches around. I think you might know one or two of them." She looked thoughtful and smiled. "I think I answered both your questions, didn't I? If not, I got here because I'm magical. A lot magical. And I'm a relative of the Fosters. You have heard of them, haven't you?"

"A grand witch. All right. And yes, I've heard of the Fosters. You'd have to be a fool not to have heard of the richest people in the world. But what does that have to do with you popping here right now? I'm assuming that you're here because of the note I received." She nodded. "Oh, good. I thought perhaps I was going before a firing squad or something. I'm not, am I?"

"Good heaven no. You're visiting a friend of the family, the president. How did I miss that you were going to be a part of the family, I wonder. Not to mention such a huge part. Did you know that…well, of course you didn't know. I would have been the only one to tell you." She asked her if she was off her meds. "That's a funny question, you'd think so, wouldn't you. But I'm trying to get it into my head that you're Kayce's mate. I didn't see that one coming."

"How could you? Unless you can see the future?" She nodded, and that was when the limo pulled up. "Are you riding with me or am I on my own for a while?"

"I'll come with you. Jeb is a friend of mine, too." They both were handed into the long, sleek limo with presidential flags on the front of it. There was an escort, too, but she didn't pay them any mind. She was still trying to work out why the witch was with her. "I'll get to that. We have about thirty minutes."

The ride was smooth as they pulled out of the parking lot to the large airport. As soon as they were on the road, Molly turned to the witch and stared at her. She was quite beautiful and seemed to glow. She figured that was her magic, if she was to believe her lore about grand witches.

"I'm truly the grand witch. My husband is the grand warlock. We have a lot of magic, and believe it or not, we get more stuff daily. I'm to help you along today, but I think I'll wait. And by the way, the glow is my white magic. I'm extremely powerful." She nodded and asked her why she was seeing the president. "You're going to be mustered out. Today. We can't have you working all the way across the United States from Kayce when he might need you. And he will if for no other reason than to get your house in order. It will need to be put into order before anything else."

"Do people understand you? I mean, so far all you've given me is bits and pieces of conversation, and I have no idea what you're talking about." She grinned at her, and Molly shook her head. "You're not the least bit funny or charming. I have asked you several times now as to why I'm seeing the president, and you've gone on about how I must have slipped under your radar or something along those lines."

"That's just what you did. You see, I knew about the other mates before they came along. I knew what day they'd fall in love with the Tucker men. They're about the best there is. I didn't see you coming along at all. I actually thought that poor Kayce wouldn't have a mate at all, you'd been so hidden from me." She asked her why it's important that she's here now. "Because you and Kayce will make all the difference in the world to…well, to the world. You two will have children who will go on in the foundation more than any other child who comes to the others."

"We haven't talked about children yet. We've talked about a lot of things, but not whether or not we're going to have kids." She said that they'd have enough to fill the bedrooms in their new home. "Eight kids is a lot of kids."

"Six. You must have a playroom for them and also one for you and Kayce. That's where you'll find it. The money to work on the house." She asked her what she was talking about. "I can't tell you everything. Just the things that you'll need to know to get you started in the right direction. You'll see when you get the bedroom cleaned up. Your grannie was a smart woman, and she knew how to save some money. There, is that enough for you to be satisfied?"

"Satisfied with what? You're still giving me bits and pieces." She looked out the window. "For all I know, this ride is something of a nightmare ride, and when I get off, I'm going to be in my bunk with the other men and women that I share with, and you'll be nothing but a bit of heartburn. I haven't ever had it before, but you could be that."

"I'm really a witch." She nodded, still not looking at the woman. "You have to believe me. I've brought you good news. Say you believe in me, and I'll show you something else that you'll need to know for your meeting with Jeb."

"Who's Jeb?" She told her, and Molly turned to look at the beautiful woman. "I'm not sure what's going on. You'll have to give me more than you have, or I'm going to believe what I should. That I'm about to be let go from the service for some unknown reason, and I'm going to be struggling to finish my Pop-pop's house for the rest of my life. Because if I don't get my check, that's what's going to happen."

"You'll finish the house and in record time because you'll be able to afford the crews needed to work on it. Also, I've told you…well, no, I didn't, but I'm telling you now that this is going to be a good thing with the meeting with Jeb. He's not known about you, but I'm bringing you to him so that he can help you out of the service before your six months are finished.

He can do that too. You've worked enough overtime that it'll be a piece of cake for him to help you out of the service with all the perks you've been waiting on." She asked about the house. "The house is going to be a showcase with you and Kayce behind the renovations. And your children will grow up to appreciate all the hard work that you've put into your lives and will be there for you forever."

"I understand that we'll find the means to do the house. Though why it would be in my granddas bedroom is beyond me. But I get you think so. Also, that we'll have six kids. Though that's another thing I don't understand. You might say I'm humoring you on that part. That's still a lot of kids to have." She nodded and told her she'd be a good mother. "Thank you for that. I don't know how I could be when I know nothing about children. I'm thinking I understand about the president and him getting me out of the service, but what does all of this have to do with me being in the service in the first place? I only have six months to go, so why not just allow me to do that bit for my country, and the rest of the stuff will fall into place?"

"You have to be home for Kayce when he needs you. So far, he's doing very well without you around. And he will continue to do so. But he will need you around just to be someone he can talk to. He's not going to have a good time in leaving the group that he's in. They'll try to drag him back, and with you around, he'll do the right thing." She asked if he would be hurt. "Physically? No. But mentally, they'll drag him down to their level, and that won't be good for the two of you. You will have your first child by the summer of next year."

They were pulling into the White House driveway when she turned to look at the woman again. She didn't understand anything that was going on. She wanted to, but didn't. Why did her getting out of the service have so much riding on it? And if she was going to have a baby by next summer, she should be starting on that, as it wasn't but ten months away. When the limo came to a full stop, they both just sat there. She had a thought that this wasn't the only thing going on with this meeting.

"You'd be right." Frustrated beyond anything she'd been frustrated about before, she got out of the car when the door was opened for her. There in the doorway stood the president of the United States with his wife standing next to him. Not sure what she was supposed to do, she waited until he made the first move. There were just too many Secret Service agents around for her to think that he was going to give her a huge bear-like hug. Though that's exactly what he did.

"Hello Molly. Welcome to your home. I say that to all the guests that I meet. It throws them off a bit." He introduced his wife to her, and she shook her hand. "There are some people here that I'd like for you to meet. And Kayce is here as well. I had to work hard in getting him to come to me, but he's here now."

Molly looked at Parker, the witch. "You had something to do with him getting here before me, didn't you?" She said her husband had. "I see. More mystery to unravel. I suppose this is where I get my job taken care of."

"Among other things." She decided that she was going to go with it. Not having any idea what she was going with, but she decided it was that or go insane. When invited into the grand building, she made her way to where Kayce was standing and took his hand into hers. Whatever happened next was going to either get them both arrested or they'd be going home together. Time would tell.

Chapter 3

The kitchen was a mess. Every place he looked, there were piles of debris. He didn't want to freak out or anything, but he was beginning to think that the house was never going to be the same and they'd never be able to live in it. He stepped outside on the covered porch and sat in the swing that was still there. He was happy when Molly decided to come out and join him.

"I'm still trying to figure out how I was able to get out of the service because of my overtime hours when I was paid for them. Also, and this one boggles my mind a great deal, we were married in the White House with about fifty guests that I didn't know. Did you know any of them?" He said that he'd met some of the Fosters but not all of them, and that was who was there. "Ronin is some kind of big deal to you, isn't he? I got that feeling when you were around him, you seemed sort of scared of him."

"He's the king of my kind. He and his wife rule us. Brook, I've talked to the most, but I know them, yes. And Parker and her husband." She told him that she was scary. "No kidding. I find her to be more scary than Ronin and Brook for some reason."

She finally sat down beside him, and he took her

hand. There was something comforting about having her close that he didn't know how to explain it. She kissed the back of his hand, and they rocked for a few minutes while the hammering and sawing went on behind them in the house. Molly finally turned to him.

"I've been through my granddas bedroom, and I didn't find anything worth all that much. There are some lovely quilts that I'd like to use on the kids' beds, but nothing that would make me think it's going to be enough to finish the house with." He said that it might be in the walls. "Then I guess we'll have to have them start on that room before we do the bathrooms. Don't you think?"

"I don't know what to think." She agreed with him on that, and they rocked some more. "What do you think about us having six kids? I mean, it seems like a lot to me, and I'm going to be carrying them. Do you think she should have told us that part? I mean, she kind of took all the surprise out of us finding out on our own. Especially the one that we're having by Christmas of next year. That's not a great deal of time, is it?"

"Do you want to have a child this soon?" Molly shrugged, and he did the same back to her. "I don't have an opinion one way or the other. It's your body, and if you want to have a child right away, I'm all for it."

"You just want to have a part in making the

baby." He said that there was that. "I see how you are. We'll have a baby by Christmas, and I guess it will be settled. Though there is a lot going on here for me to suddenly have a baby. The house is a mess. Did you think it would be like this when you and I decided that the kitchen needed to be taken down to the studs and rewired? I certainly didn't."

"My offices are worse than in here. They had to take down walls so that they could put them back up with more power running through them." He looked in the direction of his new offices and thought of how Molly had saved him a lot of heartache when he'd left the group. "I'm so glad you were there when I had to deal with them. They were saying that I had not worked out my contract. If you'd not gone over it the night before, I would have been scrambling to find the part where I had to give them sixty days' notice, and you knew right where it was. I would have been devastated to know that I had to work another sixty days with them. Thank you for that."

"It was something that the witch said." He called her by name. "Yes, that's it, Parker. She told me that I'd be helpful when it came time for you to leave. I'm just glad that I went over your contract when I did. And that you had stapled your letter of resignation to the back of it. I might not have had that if you'd not been so good about keeping them together."

They swung some more, and he was just getting

to the point where the noise in the background was getting too much when Molly stood up. She wanted to see how his buildings were coming along. He decided that going with her would be better than hearing the house being demolished right in front of them. They'd go see his offices, having the same thing done.

"It looks like the wiring is finished." He could see where the new wiring was sticking out of the new drywall, and there were places for plugs. "You're going to have a lot of plugs in the walls. I hope that's normal."

"I have quite a few things that will need to be plugged in. Mostly they'll be used for equipment, but I will have extra if I need them." The two of them were careful where they walked. "The reception area is looking like it's coming along, too. I've already decided that I'm not going to take the nurse from the practice where I was. She and the other nurses were too tight, and I have a feeling that she'd be telling them everything that's going on here. Look at this. I love the waiting area. They were able to use most of the woodwork from the old building, like I wanted."

He would have his own office, of course, plus one where he could talk to patients when necessary. There would be six rooms set up for his patients to be seen in, and he had some equipment for the reception area that was going to make appointments and keep track of records. There would be three bathrooms set up in the place. One set for his nurses and himself, the other two would be for patients. He wanted privacy when he went to the bathroom and didn't mind paying a little extra so that he could have that. Kayce pointed out the things that were going to be in the reception area and what kind of computers he was thinking of buying so that things would be up to date from the very start.

"I want to keep my records on the computer as well as hard copies. They did that at the other place, and I kind of liked having a copy of everything that was in the records that they kept." She said that she had a scanner that she used to download all her receipts onto the computer so that she could keep track of them. "Good idea. We'll have to start doing that for the house when it gets finished."

"Do you think it will get finished?" He said that he had faith in the system. "I'm glad that one of us does. All I can see is a mess. I'm afraid to bring pop-pop around. He'll have a heart attack over what we've done to his house."

"I've been showing him pictures, not of the messes but of the offices that I have going in. He is having a good time telling me what my offices need over other offices. He said there should be up-to-date magazines around instead of them being years old. I promised him that I'd take care of that." They both laughed, and she waited to see what one of the workers was going to be doing with the drywall that he had in his hands. "I didn't know they were that far along in the process. I thought that it would be another month before they were ready to hand drywall."

"I think that they're getting the rooms done first. It'll be chilly soon, and they can work on the bigger rooms all together. That's what I see anyway." They were excited to have something getting done, and the foreman said that's what they were doing. Getting one room at a time done so that they could see progress. "I love being able to see what's going to happen here. It's like the entire building is going to be done right when I can see one of the rooms finished up."

"I agree." They made their way back to the house and saw that the workers were putting in the wiring. They would have an ample amount of plugs along the countertop so that they could plug things in, like a coffee machine and other items, as they needed. The large center work area was going to be big enough that it could be used as a table if necessary, and he was excited to see that going in, too. They were headed to the bedrooms when he remembered about the find they were supposed to get.

"I have no idea what it could be. I've spoken to your grandda, and he said that his wife was forever saving things for a rainy day. It might well be in one of the hat boxes. He said that he'd never gotten around to getting rid of her things yet, and it might be in one of them." She told him that she looked into the boxes but didn't find anything but hats. "I guess we'll have to wait until we get started on the room, then. I just hope that we find something. The kitchen alone is going to cost us a fortune. I know that we have the loan that we need, but we might be paying on it until we're old and gray."

They both thought that was funny. She'd been told that she was an immortal now and didn't know how she felt about that. To outlive everyone around them would be hard. She'd just have to wait and see what happened in the future. Right now, all she could think about was how much it was costing them to have a nice house. It was a good thing there were no house payments to begin with. That might have ruined them with their money coming in. She was getting her full retirement package, but that wasn't enough to renovate the whole house without having a bit extra. She was worried about money, but Kayce said they were fine. She hoped so. She didn't want to lose the house now that it was getting into shape.

They'd been staying in his condo since the house was being torn apart. It was actually too small for the two of them, but they were making it work. They'd been sleeping together since they'd gotten back from DC and were getting some solid eight hours of sleep. She didn't think too much about having sex with Kayce. They'd get to it when they could.

She's never been one who enjoyed sex all that much. The few times that she'd had it, things hadn't been as epic as she thought they were supposed to be. She wanted to blame it on the men, but each of the three men that she'd slept with hadn't fulfilled their end of the bargain. Perhaps she was waiting for the right man to come along. She didn't know, but wasn't looking forward to disappointing Kayce when he was being so nice about not pushing her into anything.

It had been a long day, and it was only one in the afternoon, but she was ready for a nap. There had been a lot going on around the house and building that she just wanted it to be finished. As soon as she was ready to go to bed for a couple of hours, her phone rang. Not knowing the number, she answered it cautiously with just her last name.

"What a way to answer the phone when you know it's your father. What are you doing with my dad? I can't seem to find him anywhere, and he's not answering his phone." She said that he'd given up his cell phone for the quiet. "I don't believe that at all. He should know that I'm trying to reach him, and he should have his phone on him at all times."

"Did it ever occur to you that he might not want to speak to you?" He said that was impossible as he was his only child. "Yet he's not answering your calls. Not that he could. I told you that he's given up his cell phone for the phone he has in his room. By the way, he's not living at the big house anymore. He's checked himself into an assisted living place that will bar you from coming near him." He said he'd just have to check himself out of it.

"I suppose you had something to do with it." She told her dad that she'd not, but was glad that he was there. "They're going to be taking his checks, I suppose. That's not going to be good for me. I need that money more than he does. I have plans today that have me using all his check. You'll have to spot him some money. Or give it to me. I could use a few grand now that we're talking about it."

"We weren't talking about it, you were. And no, I'm not going to be giving you money. I don't have any to spare for you. Why don't you get a job? It might go a long way in making sure you have your own Social Security checks when you get to be sixty-five. Not that I care if you live that long." He sputtered around for several moments, and she had to stop her own laughter. It wasn't often she got the better of him, and it felt good. "How are you not in jail? I thought I pressed charges against you that would have you there for a little while. At least until the judge came around and sentenced you."

"I'm using my one call to call you to see where my father is. And since you were no help at all, I want you to get your skinny ass down to the station house and get me out of here. This is no place for a man like me, and I want out." She told him that it sucks to be him. "You're going to pay for that, see that you don't. I'm sick of fucking around with you right now."

"Good, because I've had enough." Closing the connection, she put her phone on the table. It was easy to feel like she'd gotten the better of him right now, but in a few hours, less probably, she'd start to worry if he'd not make good on his promises. "Time will tell, I suppose."

~*~

It took him three hours to put together his desk. It was well worth it, but he'd never imagined that it would take him that long. As soon as he pulled his chair out of the box, he knew that he was going to be sore tomorrow from crawling around on the floor getting things done. It wasn't like his office was done in the new building, but it was close enough that they told him that he could do things like this to get a start on opening his offices. Kayce was getting excited to see some results of the labor that was going on around him and was happy that they had started out the house on the right route. The kitchen was something that they'd use daily, and he wanted it to be finished first.

As soon as he finished his chair, Molly came out to see him. She'd been popping in and out for the last several hours, and he thought that she was bored. He could find her something to do, but he wanted to know that she was well rested first. The last couple of weeks had been hard on the two of them, and he, for one, was glad for the extra sleep he was getting. Having her beside him was a wonderful feeling that he thought he could get used to.

"I just had a call from my dad. He's pissed off because pop-pop is in a nursing home and not making it, so he can steal his checks. He also demanded that I come down there and bail him out, but I found that I like him being in jail. It's one less thing that I have to worry about." He said it made him and his lion feel better about him being there as well. "Do you want to have sex with me? Before you answer that, I'm not sure you'll enjoy it all that much. I'm not very good at it, and I really could care less if we have it. I've had a couple of people tell me that I'm cold."

"That's not a very good recommendation. But in answer to your question, yes, I'd love to have lots of sex with you. I think that whoever told you that you weren't very good at it didn't know what they had." She told him that it had been a couple of the men that she'd had sex with. "Like I said, they didn't know what they had. I will worship you and feel like the luckiest man in the world to have you beneath me."

"I don't know about all that." She sat down on the edge of his desk and looked sad. "I'm sure we need to have sex sooner rather than later because of the baby and all. Perhaps the next room we have done will be a nursery, so that we're ready. Again, I'll tell you that I know nothing about babies, much less ones that will change into a lion someday."

"I don't either. I'm the baby of the family, and until my brothers have their own children, I don't think I'm going to get much in the way of experience with them either. I'm a little too old to be thinking about babysitting now." She asked him about his practice. "There is that, but they're not mine, so I have no idea how to even change a diaper. The moms usually do that after I examine the babies."

"But you have more knowledge than I do. And that's good. I've heard that the parents always screw up their first child. Do you suppose that's true?" He said that he didn't think that was right. "I don't know. Anyway, how about when the crews are gone, we have some sex? That way, if I'm ready, we'll have one more thing off our list of shit that needs to be taken care of. The way that I figure it, if I get pregnant soon, the baby will be here right about July. That's still summer, and that will be good for us."

"I wish she'd not told us about the baby. It makes making one so sterile. Don't you think?" She said that she'd hoped to get to plan out when she had a child, but this just made it seem like they were on a timed schedule. "I know just what you mean. But baby or no baby, I'll gladly make love with you. I haven't told you this yet, but I have fallen in love with you. I think I have loved you since I showed up at your house and we shared a meal together. Our first of many, I hope."

"I'd like to go out to dinner sometime, too. We've been living together for two weeks now and are married. We've never even had our first date." He said that he could plan something for them. "I'd like that. Someplace fancy with cloth napkins. And I like nearly every kind of food out there and am willing to try just about anything that I've not eaten. I heard that your brother Jack has a good place to go. Would you like to go there some night?"

"He does have cloth napkins." They both laughed, and he pushed his chair up to his desk. "All they need to do in this room is paint, and it'll be finished. I've decided not to have carpet in this room as it will be harder to clean. Plus, I think that carpet holds germs more than a hardwood floor."

"I love the floor in this room. And you're right, it would be harder to keep clean with people going in and out of it all the time. I heard from one of the workers that two of the rooms are finished. It won't be long, and you'll be able to start seeing patients soon. I bet you can't wait to get started."

The two of them talked about his schedule when working, and she told him that she was going to have to get herself something to do. He suggested the foundation a couple of days a week, which is what he worked, and they could perhaps work the same schedule.

"All I do is answer the phone and take notes on why they've called. Then, after they have the forms filled out to get some money, there is a big criterion for them to get it so that we're not just giving money away, we as a family take a vote or sort of on who will receive funding." She said she could do that. "Good. I'll talk to my brothers and get you put on the schedule. It's not that hard. No one can enter the building with ill will in their heart. We learned that the hard way."

On the first day they were to open, someone came with enough firepower to take out everyone in the building, including the people who had been waiting in line to receive help. If not for the fast thinking of one of the sisters-in-law, Bailee, Denver would have been dead and several hundred other people as well.

The man had been off his medication, and no one was checking on him to make sure that he was all right. Instead of him taking out the entire building of people, he was the only one who had died, and it had been sad for Bailee to have had to kill him. But it was him or everyone there.

After getting dressed up, they decided to go to dinner tonight. When they came home, he had plans for his little wife, and he wasn't going to be disappointed in her at all. How could he be when he loved her with every fiber of his being? As soon as he called Jack and got permission to use the table that he had there for when family came in, they made their way there to have some comfort food. The fried chicken was the best he'd ever eaten, and he felt like he could eat an entire platter all to himself. He was glad that the food was served family style. That way, he could have as much food as he wanted without having to wait for a second plate of food.

Jack had been using the recipes that they'd all grown up with. Grannie, the best person in the world who had raised them, had been taking care of them since he was about three years old. She was the only mother figure that he'd ever known and felt like she was the best role model that he'd ever had. He didn't know what he was going to do when she passed on. She and grandda had been the glue that held them all together when things had gotten bad back in Texas. Which wasn't all that often, but enough that he never went without if he had the money for it. Also, it taught him how to save money when he had it so that when a rainy day came along, he would be prepared for it. He thought that was why he was so good at investing for his future, because of his grandparents.

After dinner, they walked home. It was a lovely night, and they were just full enough that they needed a nap. He'd been lying down for the last couple of days to take a little nap, and it had done him a world of good. Just today, he'd laid down for an hour and got up so refreshed that he was able to not just put his desk together with the chair but also some of the cabinets in his office that he was going to keep his notes in. They were in the kitchen when he realized that all the cabinets had arrived.

"I bet they have them in tomorrow. The floor looks good now that it's been sanded, don't you think?" She said it was hard to tell with all the stuff laying around, but she thought she'd love it when it was cleaned up. "I think you had a wonderful idea in just sanding it down instead of replacing it. I think that the rest of the floors will be just as good-looking when they're finished."

"How did they get to this point so fast, I wonder. I mean, it's only been a couple of weeks since they started, and they're already putting in the cabinets." He told her what Parker had said to him when he'd asked too. "So they're all faeries that are working on the house and the outbuilding. I never would have guessed that. I guess they'd have enough magic that they could do just about anything they wanted quickly."

"When no one is around, they use their considerable magic to get things done that normally would have taken days. That's why I've been staying out of the rooms that they're working on. Someone has already started working on the bedrooms upstairs, so that they'll be finished soon, too." She asked him about the master bedroom. "I'm going to have Parker come over and explain what she meant about finding some kind of treasure. It might be something that gets destroyed while the room is being redone, and I don't want that. She said she'd come over tomorrow afternoon to show us. She said that she'd told us too much when she'd been talking to you and wants to make up for it."

"Good. That'll take a load off my mind. I'd like to go through the room and get rid of some of the things that grandda left behind, but like you said, I'm afraid of destroying something that is valuable. Or tossing it out. For all I know, it could be one of the million lottery tickets that she's saved over the years. I thought about going through them. I did notice that one or two of them are worth some money, but I don't think they all are. At least I don't think so." He asked if some of them expired. "They do. I had to look that up myself. You have about a year after the game ticket has expired before you can't cash it out. Grannie's been gone for about two years now, so unless pop-pop is doing the same thing, then I'm doubting that it's in the tickets."

"Whatever it is, I hope that we can use it without causing any trouble. I'm thinking that if we do get a windfall, your family is going to expect it coming to them." She said she'd not thought of that, but he was right. "We'll have to think of a way so that they don't find out. I'm all for that. I mean, we are getting the house done, and that's taking about all our funds, but what do we tell him if we suddenly have a great deal of money?"

"Nothing. The less he knows, the better. And perhaps with all the shit he's done in the last year or so, they'll all spend some time in jail where they should be anyway. Isn't there some kind of law that says that you can't steal someone's Social Security check? If not, then there should be one. Pop-pop has to fight them every month for him to be able to pay his bills. Not to mention knocking him around like he's not related to them."

"I'll ask Ivy or Hudson. You've met them, haven't you?" She said that she had. "Good. Hudson is the stay-at-home dad right now, and Ivy works for the foundation. She's really good. They both are, so we keep on top of things like that in the event something comes back to bite us in the ass. She is the one who went over my contract with the group that I worked with. She told me not to sign, but I was desperate for a job and signed it anyway. I'm so glad that I got them out of my hair."

They talked about all kinds of things as they toured the house. It really was coming along nicely, and he could see them moving in sometime soon. More than likely in the next month or so. As soon as they started back to the house, he decided that he was going to prove those other men wrong about Molly and give her the best night of sex that he could. She was his everything, and he was going to prove it to her.

Chapter 4

William didn't know why his daughter was too haughty all the time. He'd raised her just like he had the boys, and she had to turn out to be the one rotten apple in the bunch. Of course, all she'd been good for was cooking and cleaning. And when she'd gotten out of high school, she up and joined the Army. She was out of reach for him for five long years, and when she returned, she was more uppity than before.

"Your lawyer is here. Do you want to talk to him here or in the conference room? Just so you know, you're going to be recorded no matter where you go." He said he'd not given anyone any permission to record him. "It's part of you being arrested. When you came in here, you were told. You even signed off on the paperwork that said you understood that it would happen. Here or in the conference room? It's entirely up to you."

"In the conference room. Is this one of those free lawyers? I don't have the money for a fancy one. Just pull someone off the street to have them with me. I'm going to win this anyway. There is no way that she should have been able to press charges on me when she's the one who put me in the hospital." He asked if she was defending herself. "I don't care what she was doing. She hit on her father, and that ain't right. I want to have her arrested for this shit."

"Watch your language. And you started it when you slapped her around. Then you used a hockey stick on her." He smiled at the memory, then remembered that she'd turned it on him. That wasn't right. "Get back against the wall."

After he'd been put in cuffs to walk down the hallway, he saw his sons. They were a sorry lot, the two of them. Sprawling around in their cells like they didn't have shit to do. They should be planning their next job, not acting like they didn't have anything to do. He looked at Seth when he told him hi.

"What are you doing? You should be planning a way out of here. Or the next job we gotta do. Money don't grow on leaves, you know? If you want something, you'd better be figuring out a way to make it happen, not sitting around on your asses and acting like it's the end of the world." He said he didn't have his phone to plan with. "Damn it, boy, don't you have a brain? What's this world coming to when a man needs his phone to get a job done?"

"I just want out of here. I thought you said that Molly was going to come through for us? I've not seen hide nor hair of her since I was put in here. The least she could do was come and see us. Give us someone to talk to. But no, she's too busy doing army shit to bother with us." He'd forgotten about her going back to the service. That did put a damper on things. "You getting out? Where are you going?"

"To see my lawyer. Do you idiots have one yet? You might need them. I'm going to see about getting out by blaming this whole thing on Molly. She had no right to knock me around like I'm not her daddy." He said that he knocked her around first. "I know that, but it won't mean a hill of beans when I get her back here. Do you suppose she'll be back in the States soon? Dad usually knows that."

He didn't know what to think about his dad being in a nursing home. He'd be getting better care, which means that he'd live longer. He wanted to get into the house so he'd have someplace to lay his head at night. Then there were his checks. They'd be taking all of it for themselves and not leaving a thin dime for him to use. People were selfish like that, he thought. Taking a man's money when he was down. He'd have to get what he needed from Molly, and she'd better be paying up, too. No more of this shit telling him no.

The lawyer looked like he wasn't even shaving yet. As soon as he sat down, he told him the rules as to what he was going to be doing for him. He didn't care for rules, but he was sure that the man had said them before. He didn't even look like he cared when he asked him about a cell phone.

"You're not to have one when you're

incarcerated. You have phone privileges once a day, so make that count." He asked how he was supposed to get in touch with him. "I'll be here when I have time and right before your court hearing. Your hearing is set for ten days from today. That should give you time to go over any notes you might have on what happened the day that you beat the young woman up."

"She's my daughter, not just some random girl I seen on the streets. That should count for something." He said it made it worse that he was beating on his own child, as far as he was concerned. "Well, it's a good thing you're supposed to be on my side, then ain't it? I want to know how I can be released on my own? They had work programs for that, don't they? Not that I plan on working, but I have shit to do, and being behind these bars isn't getting anything done."

"You'll have ten days to figure out a job for yourself. I'll be bringing you a newspaper so that you can look for one." He said again that he didn't want to work. "Then you'll be in jail for that much longer. You'll have to have employment, or you won't be released. That's the way things go."

"You don't have much in the way of good news for me, now do you?" He said his job was to try to keep him out of jail. Beyond that, he just didn't care. "Are you going to help me all that much? You don't seem old enough to even be out of high school, much less the colleging that you had to do."

"I'm a board-certified attorney, which should be enough for you." He didn't like him and told the man that. "I don't care. It's not like we're going to be pen pals when this is over. You just figure out a job that you can go to when you get out, or not. Whatever you do won't reflect on me whatsoever. But we have court in ten days, and you'd better have a good reason why you beat your daughter nearly to death, from what I've heard."

"She lived more to my shame." The lawyer was making notes, but he didn't care. It wasn't right that Molly had more rights than he did. "Do you think you can sue her for me? She beat me so badly that I had to stay in the hospital for five days before I could get around. Somebody taught her how to fight dirty, too. That ain't right."

"She's in the service, I heard. They more than likely taught her how to do hand-to-hand combat to defend herself." He asked if they really taught her how to fight hand-to-hand like that. "I would imagine. She would have all kinds of training to make sure that someone didn't get the better of her. She more than likely can carry a gun now, too, to defend herself. You might want to keep that in mind the next time you encounter her. She's going to be dangerous to be around."

"There's no way that she'd shoot her dad." He told him that he would if he had to defend himself against someone bigger than him. "She's a little bitty thing, my daughter, but like I said, she fights dirty. Like she knew just where to punch me when I was down." The man didn't say anything but continued to make notes on shit. William thought of something that he needed. "How do I get me a pencil and paper to use while I'm waiting for my day in court? I could use it to find me a job, too."

"I have a newspaper for you now that you can look in. And a pencil that you can borrow right now, but I'm going to get it back from you before I leave." He handed him the smallest pencil he'd ever seen and the newspaper section that was devoted to jobs. "You need to at least make it known that you're job hunting and have an interview with a place of employment before the court date."

"I'll look, but I'm not going to find nothing. Who is going to hire someone in jail? Nobody. That's why I don't have me a job in the first place." It was a lie. He'd never worked a day in his life and wasn't planning on getting a job either if he could help it. "What does it mean here that they'll hire most anyone that has a driver's license? I have one, but it's been expired longer than I think I knew how to drive."

"How have you been getting around?" He told him he had a car, didn't he? "I have no idea what you have or don't have, but if you're driving on an expired license, then that's going to be more trouble than just beating up your daughter."

"We won't tell him that part then. I'll just have to make do like I usually do. My dad has some checks coming to me. When can I expect them to get to me?" He asked what kind of money that his father owed him. "His monthly check. Usually, I just go over and get them, but he's in a nursing home now, and I didn't give them permission to take them from me. He's all right to be in there; my daughter can pay for that. But I have plans for his check every month, and that don't mean he gets to spend it on himself."

"You take your father's Social Security check each month?" He said only when he can get to the mailbox before he does. "You steal it right out of his mailbox? Do you have any idea how bad that is? You can go to prison just for that. And please don't tell me that you knock him around for it when he gets to it before you do."

"When he's being selfish by taking it out of the mailbox before I can get to it, I might have to beat him up a little bit. What's wrong with that? He doesn't need it. He should have died a long time ago. And don't think that I'm not tempted to help him along with that too sometimes." The man jerked the pencil right out of his hand and started putting his things back in the case he'd brought with him. "What's wrong with that? It's not like anyone cares what an old man is doing when he gets the shit beat out of him. Dad should know better than to take something that doesn't belong to him."

"It *does* belong to him. He worked hard to earn that money, and you're the one being selfish by taking it from him." He didn't see it that way and told him so. "I can't work with you. I thought that this was going to be a simple case of just beating your daughter. Not that that's bad enough, but you've admitted to driving on an expired license and stealing a government check right out of the mailbox. Not to mention beating the man up for it when he got to his money before you were able to steal it from him. That's a federal crime punishable by up to ten years in prison as well as fines up to a quarter of a million dollars. I hope you think that's worth it. I'm leaving before you admit to killing anyone. I wouldn't put it past you."

He was out the door before he could tell him that he'd actually murdered some people, but he had done his jail time for that and was no longer guilty when he did it again. He had a free pass to that since he knew that he'd been in prison before. That was when he realized that not only did he not have the newspaper, but he didn't have any way of making notes when he had an idea on how to make money. The man was loony if he thought that he'd been a saint all his life.

When he was taken back to his cell, he saw his sons sitting in the same position they'd been sitting in before. The only difference that he could see was that they were both asleep now instead of just lying there. Damned kids. He couldn't figure out why he'd had three of them when just one would have been too much.

Back in his cell, he thought about the lawyer not being fair in his questions. When he'd asked him something, he should have expected a truthful answer. Wasn't that how he was going to get him out of here? He didn't know how he was supposed to get a job now when he'd taken the paper. Not that he was going to try all that hard, but it was something that he was going to pretend to do anyway.

And why was he so fired up about his dad's check? It wasn't like everyone didn't steal their parents' checks. He could count on both hands and his toes on how many people he knew had them mailed directly to them when their parents were dead. That's what he was hoping to do with his dad's checks. Get them long after the old fucker was dead. He wondered how he was going to get the checks now that his attorney had bailed on him. That just wasn't right. People should be more forthcoming when it comes to checks in the mail.

Lying down on his cot, he thought about how much his dad got from the social office. He'd been getting more lately and wondered who he was going to have to take care of to get another raise on them. Something that he was going to ask his next attorney. If one came. That one had his panties in a twist about something before he left.

~*~

It was nearly nine o'clock when they made their way back to the condo. They'd toured the whole house again and were surprised to find that two of the bedrooms on the second floor were finished. It would take longer for the master to be done because they were making changes on it all the time. They just needed to stick with a plan and be done with it. However, he did like the idea of having all new windows around the room. And the fireplace had needed to be cleaned up before they could use it.

"Do you suppose that once the house is finished, it'll be magical? I read that in a book one time about how faeries lived in the house and would do things around it so that the owners didn't have to even make the beds. I hate making the bed." He said that he didn't enjoy it either when it was just going to be messed up again. "That's my thoughts too. I guess we have to make it when we get up so that it's not messy when we get back in it. I do not care for a messy bed when I'm going to sleep."

"You're as odd as I am." They both laughed, and he pulled her into his arms. "Do you still want to make love with me? It's late, but that doesn't matter to me."

"I want you. I want to have sex with you all night. Do you suppose that will be enough time for us to get comfortable with each other?" He grinned at her, and she smiled back. "You look hungry. Is that you or your lion? I'd like to know."

"Both of us want you; however, I'll be the only one who has sex with you. He'd be too rough with you and would hurt you." She pulled her blouse out of her pants and started unbuttoning it from the bottom up. "I'd love to see you naked before me. Take all your clothing off so that I can marvel at what's mine."

"I'm strong. I have to run every day and lift weights to keep in shape while I'm in the service. I wonder what I'll do now." Her blouse was off, and she dropped it to the floor. "I find that I really enjoy wearing nice silk next to my skin when no one knows." The bra was bright pink and had a little rose in the front of it. When she undid the front clasps, he watched as she pulled it off the front of her, holding it in place like she was teasing him. He was enjoying that as much as he knew he'd love making love to her. "I love the way you look at me. It makes me wet with anticipation."

Kayce watched as she undid her pants. They were just jeans, but they molded to her body like a second skin. He licked his lips, thinking of the treasures that she was hiding beneath them. As soon as she bent to take them off, he lifted her up from the floor and turned her to the wall. He couldn't wait much longer.

Taking her mouth, he kissed her with all the passion that he had stored up for her. She gave as good as she got, and he loved her for it. Once he pulled her panties off her, the same bright color as the bra had been, he tossed them to the floor. Dropping to his knees, he opened her nether lips and suckled her clit into his mouth and flicked it with his tongue. Her climax flooded his mouth with her cream, and he lapped every bit of it down.

"Fuck me." He wanted to do just that, but he was enjoying eating her too. When she yanked his head from her pussy, he looked up at her. Her eyes were dazed-looking, and she looked at him hungrily. It was all he could do not to fist himself and come right where he was sitting. "Please, fuck me. I need to feel you deep inside of me."

Standing up, his knees weak from all the blood going to his cock, he pressed her against the wall and ate at her mouth. Once he got his pants undone with her help. He didn't bother with pulling them down very far, but slammed deep inside of her quickly. As soon as she screamed out her release, he fucked her hard.

Nothing could have prepared him for the way it felt to be deep inside of his mate. She wrapped her legs around his hips, and he took her deeper. When she came again, he decided that he was going to take her to the couch where he could make love to her body. Lifting her up by her ass, he made his way to the couch to make love to her there. Lying her down on the couch, following her to the prone position, he continued to make love to her mouth while he pulled his pants the rest of the way off. He was in such a state of need that he wasn't sure he was going to make it until they were both naked.

Slowing down a bit, he touched her breasts and was excited when her nipple tightened under his fingers. They weren't large, but they were responsive to his touch, and he couldn't have been happier. As soon as he was able to lean down to take the small morsel into his mouth, he felt his body respond to hers, and he felt his balls fill, and his cock stiffen even more. He wanted to come. Needed to come hard with her, and he brought her over again just as his cock released.

His body felt turned inside out when he came. As he was making sure that she came as well, his body responded to her climax, bringing him over again. The third time he came, he threw back his head and roared, his lion feeling the climax as if it were coming as well.

Dropping a top of her, he couldn't have moved if he tried. The couch wasn't all that wide, so there wasn't much room for him to roll to his side anyway. When she struggled to get out from under him, he was sure he was crushing her; he rolled over and fell off the couch. When she joined him on the floor, he held her in his arms. Touching her wherever he could, he closed his eyes and waited for his heart to stop pounding. If he didn't know better, he would swear that he'd had a heart attack. Just as he was getting his breath back, she looked up at him.

"I was wrong." He said that she'd never been wrong since he'd known her. "Good one. But it must have been the men. That was the best sex I've ever had, and I want you again. Just not right now."

"No, I don't think I can stand up, much less have sex again. But I don't think that in all my life I've ever enjoyed coming with you as much as I did that last time. I think maybe I might have broken something." She laughed and laid her head back on his chest. "I love you, Molly Tucker. I can't imagine a world without you by my side."

"I love you as well." She snuggled down onto his chest, and he could feel the moment that she fell asleep. Closing his own eyes, he laid there thinking about what they'd just done. He'd have to tell her that she'd been ovulating and that they more than likely created a child tonight. He was excited about that, but was cautious too. A child would mean so much more than they had going on right now, and he only hoped that they could handle it all.

Dozing off every so often, he cried out when she kneed him when she got up. Giggling at what she'd done, she got up to use the bathroom. Lying there for a bit longer, he had to get up as well. Once he was standing, careful not to fall over, he made his way to the bathroom as well. She was just coming out when she said that she needed a shower. He told her about the baby.

"I just knew she was going to be right. Takes all the fun out of it if you ask me. At least she didn't tell me what it would be. So we do have that." Kayce joined her in the shower, and they made love again against the shower tile. "You keep this up, and we're both going to be old before our time. But I do feel much better after having sex. It's like the best medicine for being relaxed that I've ever felt."

They dried one another after getting out of the shower. Molly blew dry her hair so it wouldn't be a mess when she got up in the morning, and he watched her. There was nothing sexier than watching a woman take care of herself, and he couldn't have been more in love with her. As soon as she deemed herself ready for bed, they just got into bed naked. He usually slept that way anyway and was happy that she didn't mind. Almost as soon as his head was on the pillow, he closed his eyes and dozed off. The last thing he remembered was thinking about how much he loved her.

Waking up, he knew that he was going to have a wonderful day. Molly was riding his cock, and when he put his hands on her hips, she smiled down at him. When he asked her if she was enjoying herself, she came hard. He watched her face as she released several more times while he held her. As soon as he could, he rolled her to her back, still with his cock hard inside of her, and fucked her. She cried out once more before she again wrapped her legs around his hips and came up off the bed with each of his downward strokes. They had a good rhythm going until she cupped her breasts and fed them to him. Biting gently on her nipple had her coming again, and he joined her. He cried out that he was coming and bit down harder on her breast, drawing just enough blood that he felt his lion roll over him. It was as if they'd both bonded with their mate, and he couldn't have been happier with the

Morning sex was better than being on the couch, and he couldn't wait until they had their own room at the house so they'd have more room on the bed. Everything about the condo was too small for them, and he was glad that Molly had decided that she wanted to live there with him.

Getting dressed for the day after another shower, he headed to the hospital to see a few patients. He only had three that were there, and he discharged two of them before leaving. He was finished with the group that he'd been in and couldn't have been happier. Being finished with them meant that he could take some time off for a change and not have to worry about being on call. They'd still call him in if it was one of his patients and they asked for him, but he was free to get things going in his offices. After leaving the hospital, he made his way to the offices to see how they were progressing.

His office was finished with the last coat of paint put on the walls. In addition to that, most of the rooms were finished as well. Things were progressing well, and he couldn't wait to get into them and start working. He realized that he needed to advertise for nurses and decided that he'd do that as soon as he got back to the condo. Kayce was disappointed that Molly wasn't there when he got there. But she had left him a note.

"I've been called into the foundation to see about working. Looking forward to having something to do. See you around dinner time." Then she signed it "love Molly".

They'd been eating out nearly every night since the renovations had started. It seemed like it had been forever, but it had only been a couple of weeks. Deciding to cook them dinner, he was handy with the microwave, he made them both stroganoff. It was about the only thing that he knew how to cook well, and it was usually pretty good. When Molly got home, he was just finishing up with the extra pans that he'd used and was drying them. Kissing her on the mouth, they sat down to dinner and ate in silence. The food was really good, and he was glad that he'd been able to get something that they both liked on the stove.

"I've been officially introduced to your grandparents. They were at the foundation when I got there. I love them both." He said that he'd thought that she'd seen them before. "They were at dinner one night, but with all the food on the table almost as soon as we arrived, I didn't get to meet them. I love them both very much. Your grandda is funny and a charmer. More so than you are, I think."

"Denver is the most like them. I think it's because he hung out with them the most. He and grandda would get their heads together and get into things." She asked about his parents. "They're both dead. Did I tell you the story about how they left us at Grannie's home one Thanksgiving and never returned for us? We found out later that they sold everything we owned so that they could get away from us. They said that having ten kids wasn't what they wanted, and they just got rid of us. Ronin, I think you met him, too. He's the king of our kind, and he took them to task when they tried to get one of us to give them money. They were killed by the pride, just the way that they should have. Being the baby, I don't remember them very well, but I do know that when we were living with Grandda and Grannie, we never went without again. There might not have been meat on the table every meal, but there was love around and that was even better."

"I love you." He told Molly that he loved her as well and was glad they were mates. Then he remembered to tell her about the baby. She was excited as he was and hugged him tightly. "I'm going to be a momma, and I can't wait. I know we knew that, but this is better than I thought it would be."

He couldn't have agreed with her more. As they went up to bed that night, he kissed her flat belly and told the baby how much he loved it already. Holding Molly in his arms, he was excited for the next part of their lives when the baby came along. Hopefully, things would be set up for them, and they'd not have so much to worry about. He wondered if that was even possible.

Chapter 5

William wanted to smack his attorney or, at the very least, shut him up. He kept telling him to plead guilty to the charges of beating his daughter so that he could get out in about six months. While that didn't seem like a long time, he wanted out right now. And this attorney had even set him up with an interview for a job that he wasn't going to work for the day after tomorrow. He tried to tell him that things weren't working out for him, and he didn't want to work, but he wouldn't listen.

At least the other guy had listened to him. He was still trying to figure out how he'd gotten out of representing him. The man was off his noodle a bit, but it didn't matter. He should have been there for him when he'd been in court. Today was his day.

During his court hearing, the boys were there too, and he was ashamed at how they looked. He would admit to anyone that he was terrified of germs. They were everywhere, but he did make sure that he was clean. Both his sons looked like they'd not had a bath in weeks, instead of the few days since mandatory showers were given. He couldn't stand to be next to them for fear of catching something from the two of them.

When the judge came into the room, he asked if he could say something first off. When given permission, he'd learned how the court system worked the first time he'd been in the room, and you didn't make the judge mad at you. It was the golden rule, he thought, and would tell anyone who asked about it. As soon as he was given permission to talk, he asked about the other lawyer.

"He said that he couldn't work with you because you've admitted things that he doesn't believe in. What did you say to him?" He said he'd only told him the truth. "He said that, too. That I should read the recording of the meeting between the two of you on the only day that he was there. I have it right here. While you wait, I'm going to go over it. If you don't mind?" He told him to have at it.

While the judge read over the transcript that had been recorded that day, he tried to think if he'd said anything that would get him into trouble. Nothing that he could think of, but the man had been sorely pissed off when he left. As soon as the judge was finished, he looked at him.

"Did you really admit to taking your father's Social Security check and beating him when he wouldn't give it up?" He said that he knew that it was something that he needed, and he'd taken it from him. "You do realize that your father worked for his monthly checks and more than likely that's all he has as income in his golden years? Don't you?"

"Molly, my daughter, should be taking care of him with his bills. She's stuck so far up his ass that it's a wonder anyone can tell them apart." He was told to watch his language. "I didn't cuss like I usually do. But he should have been dead a long time ago, and I'd be getting his checks free and clear. Speaking of which, can you tell me how I can apply for more money? It's not bad, but it could be more is what I'm thinking."

"You do understand that it's against the law for you to be taking his checks, don't you? I mean, you even admitted to beating him when he didn't hand it over to you." He said he'd beat him to the mailbox, and he'd have to wait until he could get him alone before he was able to get his checks sometimes. "What about Molly? She's the one who you beat to get you into jail in the first place. Did she have a check that was supposed to come to you, too?"

"She might have some money coming in when she's in the service. I never thought to ask her about that. But no, I didn't beat her over a check. She told me no, she wasn't going to be paying me any money, and that made me mad. She should know better than to tell her own daddy no when he tells her something. She's my daughter and should want to help me out." He just stared at him. "You look like you agree with me. I can understand that if you have any kids. They're the ruination of the world if you ask me. I have them two boys over there, and they're forever getting out of helping me when I have a plan."

"What's your plan now that your father is in an assisted living place? I'm sure they're taking his checks when they come in for room and board." He said he'd been working on a plan to get him out of the place. "So you can get his checks."

"That's right. Now you understand." He smiled at the judge, thinking that he'd like to have him around all the time when he was in trouble. He understood him when he had a plan. "I don't know why they'd take his check anyway. I mean, it should be circulating around town to invest in the community. I read that one time when I was cashing the check. What are they going to do with it other than to make sure he's got three meals a day and a roof over his head? That's the reason that I need it. So I can have the comforts of home, too. Dad should have been dead a long time ago, as I said. It sure would make it easier for me to get his checks when they'd come directly to me instead of him first. It's just not right. You understand that now, don't you?"

"Why don't you have a job? I'm sure that you're able-bodied to work at one. Or your sons, for that matter? You should all three have gainful employment instead of stealing checks from someone who clearly needs it." He waved him off, telling the man that a job is for suckers. "I see. So you're too busy planning your next big thing to bother with a job that would give you three meals a day and a roof over your head. I wouldn't think that it would be enough money for the three of you to live like kings."

"I don't share with my boys. They can fend for themselves. Besides, he's my daddy, ain't he? They're going to have to find their own sucker to scam. Not my daddy." He was a little offended that he'd suggested that he share his money. "You never did tell me how I get a little more money on his checks. It sure would come in handy to have about a couple of grand more than he's getting. It doesn't go as far as it used to, and I'm hurting a little by the end of the month before the next check comes in. I can't buy me some beer that I'm craving and have some pies delivered to where I'm staying."

"Where is it that you reside?" He didn't know what that meant and had to ask. "Where are you living right now? Besides the jail system. Do you have a permanent address?"

"I'm going to be moving into my dad's old place. I'm not sure where he's going to be staying after you tell them to take him out of the nursing home place, but I've had my eye on that place for a lot of years." He asked for the address. "I don't know the exact address, but it's called the Todd Manison. Used to be called something else when my grannie was alive, but since she's dead, I've decided to call it after myself."

He turned and asked the bailiff something, and when he stepped away, William thought for sure that by this time next month, he was going to have a bigger check and a place to live. He wouldn't allow the boys to stay with him unless they proved that they could help take care of the place. He wasn't going to have them bringing in their germs if he didn't have to. Besides, it had been his daddy's place, and there was no reason why he would not be living there. That made him think of all the things that he could do to the old place. Kind of spruce it up a bit. The place was old, but it was his since his daddy had moved out of it. The bailiff came back and whispered something to the judge. He was going to have to remember his name if he wanted things to go his way from now on.

"The house that you're referring to is called Tucker Mansion as of last week. And up until then, it had been in your daughter's name. She owns it, not your father." He said that wasn't right. That he was his son. "Regardless, it won't be someplace where you can live. I'm to understand that they're having renovations done to it as we speak. I'm afraid you'll have to find some other place to live while your father is in the assisted living place."

"Do you believe that shit? She tells me no about giving me money, but she's all right with having my place done up. Why the hell is it called Tucker anyway?

That's not a name that I know." He told him that they were married, Kayce Tucker and Molly Tucker. "No. She's not supposed to be getting married. She's in the service. I know that because she comes home dressed in a uniform and wears a gun. They taught her how to fight, too, which I'm none too happy about. She nearly made me stay in the hospital for a week when she fought back when I was showing her some manners."

"As enlightening as it's been talking to you, I have a full day ahead of me, so I'm going to put you in for a court date." He asked if he'd be able to get out today; he had stuff to do. "No. I don't think I want you to be out where you can cause more trouble. I'm going to have you sent to prison until such time as a court date can be given to you. Once you have that, I'll keep you there in the event that you try to take on the government and get a raise in your father's checks. That's not going to happen either. I'm also going to have you put in prison for mail fraud, abuse of the elderly, and cashing a government check when it doesn't belong to you. There are more that I'm sure that I can tack onto that, but for now, that should be enough to keep you in jail until such time as the courts can see you again."

"Wait. I thought that you understood me. Like we was buddies of something." He said that he didn't usually become friends with convicts. "I did my time. You can't hold that over me no more. I get a free pass on killing too because of that."

"Have you killed since you got out of prison, Mr. Toby?" He said that he had, but he couldn't hold that against him. "Why not? Just because you paid for that one crime doesn't mean that you get a pass to kill again. It's against the law."

"I know that, but I served my time. I got out, and they said that I didn't have to worry about paying for that crime again. I remember thinking that was a good thing to know. That's why I call it a free pass. You can't put me in prison for the same crime." He explained to him what it meant. "No, that's not right. If that were true, then everybody I know would be back in prison for killing people again. You have to look that up. I think you're wrong about that. I can't be tried for the same crime. They told me that."

"You can't be tried for the same person that you killed. But there will be a whole new trial for the next person you kill. There are no free passes on murder. You'll have to be tried again and again for murder for as many times as you do it." He told the judge that wasn't fair. "Fair or not, that's the way it works. How many people have you killed with this supposed free pass? More than two? Three?"

"Three, but I'm not going to tell you about them if you can try me again. That's just not right. They should explain that better when a person gets out of jail." He said that he thought everyone understood that it was just him. "I still don't know how they can try a man for killing again when he paid his dues. I did too. I paid them all when I was in there. I don't want to go back to prison for any reason. It's not fair that I'm the only one being punished for this. I've known men who come out and kill someone on the same day, and they're still running around."

"I don't suppose you'll tell me who they are, would you?" He asked if the rule would apply to them getting out on the same deal. "Of course, they'll go back to prison. You just tell me who they are and I'll take care that they too understand that murder is a crime each time you do it."

"It's still not fair. I shouldn't have to be punished because someone told me wrong." He asked again about the person, and William told him, even the name of the victim. "I suppose they're going to have to understand this, too. I think someone needs to make this more clear when they let you out. There's no telling how many people I would have killed by not understanding the law. I just don't get it."

William might well have protested more had he been thinking. But all he could remember was that someone had lied to him about going back to prison. He might well have to remember that when he's set up with a bad person. Getting himself locked into the van that he'd come here in, he asked about where he was going. They told him he was going to prison just like the judge said.

"He ain't as nice as I thought he was. Sending me to the big house when I didn't know that I could get back there. And for murder, too." He was still fuzzy on the details about getting his daddy's checks and making them be more, but he'd get to that. Someone somewhere would have him some answers, and he'd get right on that. A bit more money coming his way would be nice when he got out of prison, he thought. Then he'd move into his daddy's old place, and it would be fit for a king. Yes, sir, he was ready for some changes in his life, starting with more money coming in.

~*~

Molly was never so happy with a hearing as she was the one that got her father put in prison again. Her brothers, too, were going to be spending more time in jail as well. As soon as they were all gone, she figured that she was going to have a nice little party and celebrate that they were all gone from her life.

"I guess your father made a spectacle of himself when he was explaining to the judge about being put in prison for murder already." She asked Joey, the officer who had come to tell her about the judgments against them, if people really thought that. "The judge he didn't think so. He told your daddy right off the bat that no one thought like he did and that everyone knew that murder was a crime that got you tried every time. Your father just didn't seem to get it."

"It doesn't surprise me. He's always worked rules around to suit himself. Once, when I was little, he had to pay my fees. Or he was supposed to. But since he didn't have the money, he said that the school should pay for them. He thought the same way about my meals there as well. He sent me to school, and the school was responsible for me during the time I was there. I have never been more embarrassed than that day in my life." He told her that he could understand that having to spend time with her father. "He's an idiot. So are my brothers. I'm guessing that the two of them understood that they can't go around murdering people because they'd gone to prison for it once."

"No. They got it. I was surprised, too, that the younger one, Seth, agreed to tell on his dad about the three people that he murdered. They didn't even have to offer him a deal; he just said he knew who they were and said he'd even tell them where the bodies were buried. I think your daddy is going to be in jail for a good long time now that his own kids are against him." She said that it didn't surprise her at all. They were all three exactly alike when it came to being smart. They weren't. "No, they're not. And the fact that your daddy asked the judge for more money coming on your granddas social security checks after your granddaddy was dead shocked us all. I think he really believes that there is a way for him to get them mailed to him while he's in jail, too."

After Joey left, she sat around the house watching the construction workers. They were doing such a good job that she was going to be surprised if they didn't have it done in the next couple of weeks. She and Kayce had eaten in the kitchen last night at the counters. They were so smooth that she could have laid down on them and not gotten hurt. The other counters had been rough and needed a good top laid on them. These were made of concrete, and she loved them.

"Mrs. Tucker, there is an issue with your bedroom. The master suite." She asked what sort of problem. "We found some money in the walls. There's quite a bit of it, too, when it comes down to it. It looks like it's been there a while, too. And there's a note with it. From your grannie."

She wanted to wait until Kayce came home, but he insisted that she go and have a look at what it was now. He was excited, she could hear it in his voice, and wondered why her grannie would be leaving her a note and not grandda. She couldn't wait to find out what was going on. With her cell phone on video, she talked to Kayce while she was getting ready to look.

"He said it's a bit of money. Quite a bit is what he said." He told her to hurry because he wanted to know as well. "I'm going. Don't rush me. I have no idea why it would be in the walls, so hopefully we'll know what it's about when I read the letter that came with it."

She was handed the missive and told that the money was still being pulled out of the wall. She could see it stacked on one of the wire rolls and knew that she wasn't going to be able to count it all in one sitting. Then she thought that if it was all ones, this was going to be a good joke on her. She picked up the first rolled stack of money and sat down on the floor.

"It's all hundreds. There are at least a hundred rolled stacks of money already out, and there is more. She said it would be a good amount of money, but I never dreamed...Kayce, we're going to be rich enough to pay off everything that we owe and then some." He asked her to read the letter to him. The workers left her then, and she was glad. If it said it was all counterfeit, she didn't want any witnesses to her shame. "It starts out with my dearest Molly."

"I knew that you'd be the one who would inherit the house and the person who would want to have things just so. It sort of got away from us, the house did, and it was too late for us to do much in the way of upgrades. I knew that you'd do this old house well when grandda left it to you."

"She thinks that grandda is gone and he left it to me. I'm so glad he's still around so that I can tell him what Grannie had done." Kayce asked if it explained where the money had come from. "I'm getting there. Hold on." She read on.

"I've always been lucky when it came to winning money. And I used that luck in having you and someone special that will be with you through all time to have yourself a nest egg. I never told your grandda about it, so he'd not let it slip to the boys. Your father would have beaten him to death for the money that I've put aside for you.

"I won three big payoffs. And of course, I took the cash for it all at one time. That way, the taxes have been paid on it from the start. You'll find the receipts there with the money, so that you have proof that I paid on it. I'd still not tell anyone that you have the money. Just bring it out when you need it so that no one knows. It's none of their business anyway." Kayce cleared his throat before speaking.

"Your grannie won all that money and put it aside. I wonder if there was a time that she needed it but didn't spend it?" Molly said that she didn't know, but didn't have too much more to read. "Then read on, my love, so that when I get home, we can bathe in the money."

She laughed and read on ahead without telling Kayce. As soon as she got to the end of the letter, she told him what it had said. She was fighting tears badly by the time she was able to get out what she'd told her.

"Grannie said that there was never a time when they needed the money more than I would. And that the reason there is so much is because she wanted us, my someone special, to have it for when we redid the house. She said she thinks that there is close to seventy million dollars here with all the lottery money that she won." She blew her nose and looked at the money still in the wall. "I wonder how she was able to get it into the wall without grandda knowing. I mean, there would have been a big hole in the drywall for her to have put this much money in there."

She found the receipts for paying the taxes on all that she'd won and put them with the letter for when Kayce came home. Even though she'd told him all about it, she knew he was going to be as surprised as she was for when he saw it. There were a lot of rolls of cash just sitting on top of a wire roll. And more in the wall still yet to be pulled out. That's when she looked around the room.

"Most of the room is finished. They were pulling this drywall out to make room for the dressers that we wanted to put in here. The floor looks fantastic." He asked her about the fireplace. "It's an ivory color, and I believe it's going to keep us warm at night. It's a lot bigger than I thought it was when we first looked at it. The drywall on either side of it has been taken out and widened for us."

She kept staring at the money, and when Kayce said he was coming home, she put her cell phone down and stared at it all. Never would she have believed, even with Parker telling them that it was quite a bit, that there was that much money in the walls. When she'd pointed it out to them a week ago, Molly had honestly forgotten about it because of the news about the baby. Getting up to look out over the front driveway when Kayce pulled in, she put her hand on her belly.

"We're not going to spoil you even though we can. You'll have a happy childhood because you'll be loved by the two of us." She could hear Kayce taking the stairs two at a time to get to her. "I love you, sweet baby."

They decided to do just what Grannie told her to do and take it out a little at a time. There was no point in flaunting the money around, but she would tell her Pop-pop. He would love the fact that his wife had saved them from a lot of rainy days.

Taking all the money out of the wall and off the roll, they put it in a large tote and put it in Kayce's office. Dragging it down the stairs had been funny for the two of them. It had weighed a ton, and she couldn't believe that they'd had to use a larger tote to put it in.

Deciding to leave it out in the open like it was nothing but another tote of books, she thought that no one would wonder about it, so it would be safe. Kayce said they'd have to talk to the workers who had found it so that they'd not say anything to anyone.

"I don't think they will. That would be bad for them to know secrets about the families that they work for and tell on them. I can see that they'd have a lot of stories about people and their finds in the walls." She said that they'd been looking for wiring when they'd removed the old drywall, and that was how they'd found it. "I think we're going to be set up for the rest of our lives with what we have. We'll invest some of it so that it doesn't run dry anytime soon. I've gotten pretty good at investing since I went away to college."

"That sounds like a good plan." They decided to have dinner in tonight, and that was fun too. With the kitchen nearly finished, the refrigerator had been put in as well as the stove and oven. The island didn't have any chairs around it as yet, but they made do by standing around it. She couldn't believe what a couple of weeks' difference had made in the whole house. She couldn't wait until it was finished, however. "We'll need to count it at some point, I suppose. Just to make sure that we don't spend it all the way down to nothing without thinking about it."

"I believe your grannie might have known just how much was in there when she said seventy million. That's a lot of money to win from lottery tickets. But she did say that she'd won a couple of big payoffs." Molly said that she remembered once her grannie winning a scratch off when she'd been about ten. "I guess she was right in saying that she'd been lucky with numbers. I wish I could have gotten to know her. She sounds like my grannie a great deal."

They talked about the money for the rest of

the evening. Tomorrow, when the construction crew came back to finish the bedroom, they'd talk to them. Kayce was still waiting for some applicants to fill out the positions in his office, but he was ready to go. As soon as the building was finished, he was going to be working on building up his clientele. She didn't think he'd have any trouble. He was a good man and a better doctor than she'd ever known. He was happy to be able to do his own hours and work at his own offices. She was happy for him as well.

Chapter 6

Ethan was enjoying his job and the perks that went along with it. He got to see Kayce whenever he was in the hospital and even got to see the others when he was off. Being head of surgery was the best job he'd had in a very long time. He smiled when he saw Kayce coming toward him.

"I was just coming to see you." They hugged as they always did when they saw one another. "I was wondering if you could put the word out that I'm taking patients. I don't know how often you do deliveries nowadays, but I'm looking for infants to start off with. I thought that since you're here all the time, you could hook me up."

"I can see what I can do about that. You should call some of the OBGYNs around here, too. Those guys would know if a patient of theirs had a pediatrician or not." He told him he'd sent out flyers to them to hand out. "Flyers? I do hope that you had one of the others do it for you. Shawn would hook you up right away if you asked her."

"I did, and she's the one who made it for me. Looks really professional too. Like I knew what I was doing." The two of them laughed. "But seriously, you'll have to come out and see my new building. It looks better than I thought it would. And the parking lot is nice and big too. I was surprised when I walked through it last night as to how much room I have, even with all the equipment there that I'll need, even for just starting out."

"I'm proud of you." He was a little bit jealous of his brother having his own doctor's offices, but he was glad too that it wasn't him. He didn't want the trouble of having to find patients to take up his time at this point in the game. "Are you going to have a grand opening? I would. Serve some little sandwiches that Jack can do up for you. I hear that Dakota and David are trying for a baby this time now that they have a successful business going."

They went into Ethan's office to talk, and he showed him around the office. It was coming along nicely since Georgie had been giving him things to hang in and put around his space. He told his little brother that he was having fun being the head of surgery.

"I can tell. I was never so happy as to see that people are working well together when I was here the other day. I had a tonsillectomy patient, and the surgeon was actually nice to me. Usually, I get the cold shoulder because I don't do my own surgeries." He told him that he was working on making sure that everyone got along. "It's working, whatever you're doing. I guess you learned that the hard way when

Abbott was here."

About six months ago, he'd had to take over a surgery when Sebastain Abbott, a surgeon who had been drunk more often than not, when he came into work, he'd had a lot to drink, and that wasn't the way things were done. He ended up beating the shit out of him when he thought that he was trying to show him up. That wasn't the case at all; he'd only been worried about the patient when he'd come into the room.

"We're doing random drug tests when staff come to work. So far, it's worked out great. Not many people complained about it as I thought they would, so I'm happy for that." He asked if he was in the lot as well. "Yes. You might be called into the office to be tested as well. I'm even in the rotation when it comes to having tests done. I'm not ruling out anyone."

"Good for you. I love that idea." They decided to have lunch together in the cafeteria. The food was usually good, and it was quiet down there this time of day. As they were paying for their meals, a table opened up and they sat there. "I've been thinking about the renovations on our house and have decided that it's much easier than I thought. Of course, the crew that's working on it is doing a fantastic job. All the bedrooms are finished, but the master and the kitchen will be done today. All they're waiting for is the stove to be inspected as it's gas, and they want to make sure that it's hooked up right."

"I never thought of that having to be inspected." They ate most of their meal before they began talking about their wives. "Shawn has been finishing up the house with Georgie. The stuff that she finds for the house is amazing. You should see my home office. It's a dream come true."

"I've seen her work. I think that when the house is finished with the things that we're having done to it, Molly is going to have Georgie finish off the finishing touches around the house. We don't have a lot of personal items, but for the things that were in the house before I moved in. William is enjoying all the pictures that we bring in when we go see him." Ethan asked how he was doing. "I swear, since he put himself in that assisted living place, he's gotten younger acting. Like he's had a new outlook on the house. Of course, it helps him that his son and grandsons are in prison right now. I can't believe that they thought it was all right to beat an elderly man up for his Social Security checks just because they wanted them."

They talked about the trial for William, his sons, and how they still get a laugh out of some of the things that he said. Ethan thought that the man was off his meds or something, believing that he was to get a free pass when it came to murdering people.

"I don't have a lot of time today to hang out. I'm sorry." Kayce told him it was fine; any time that he got to spend with his family was good. "Thank you for saying that. I miss you guys even though I get to see you nearly every day."

"I know what you mean. I saw Denver this morning, and it felt like it had been weeks since I saw him when it had only been a couple of days. I love you guys so much." They hugged again as they parted ways, and Ethan wanted to cancel his day just so he could hang out with his brothers. They were going to have to get together soon, all of them, to catch up. It had been a while since they had had their weekly dinners together, what with everything they were all into nowadays.

He had two meetings that he had to attend, then he had to go and watch a new surgeon. He didn't really have to, but he wanted to see how he treated the staff that was in place. He wanted people working for him who could get along with everyone. While he knew that was impossible, he also knew that seeing how they treat the nurses was a big deal to him. They were the lifeline of the hospital, and he dared anyone to say anything differently.

Going home at six, he was ready to call it a day and take a much-needed nap. Shawn would have dinner ready when he got there, and he loved her for that. Today, she'd had to have some workers finish the fence that was surrounding their house as a tree had fallen on it during the last storm. She could have fixed it herself with her magic, but like the rest of them, she was trying to put as many people to work as they could. The house was no exception. She greeted him at the front door when he got home.

"I've been thinking about you all day." He said that he'd done the same, then told her how he'd gotten to see his brother. "That's wonderful. I had lunch with Bailee today. She and Denver are planning a trip next month to go to Vegas. I hope they have a wonderful time."

"Denver will be worried about how much money they'll lose if they play any games. He's always been a worrier about money and stuff." She told him how she'd gotten that when she spoke to him about it. "One of my brothers who would enjoy something like that is Lance. He loves games of chance. I think that's why he does so well in the stock market. He's not afraid to take chances when he invests."

"Speaking of investments, I have to go over ours tomorrow. I've been so busy that I've been putting it off in favor of hanging out with you." He asked her if that was a bad thing. "No. It's the perfect reason to put things off. I love being with you."

After dinner of curry chicken and naan, they sat in the living room to watch some television. He must have been dozing some because when he woke up, the news was on. He'd slept through the entire night. Wondering if he was going to be able to sleep tonight, he undressed and got into bed. His body was so tired that he had to let it calm down a bit before he was able to rest. As soon as Shawn turned off the light, he was gone. He must have needed it because he didn't think that he was ever going to get up again.

Whistling the next morning, he was glad that he felt so much better. Getting up a little later than he'd thought that he would, he was out of the shower and dressed at a little after seven. Since he had to be to work by eight, he knew that he'd just have enough time for a good breakfast and a hug and kiss from his wife before he was out the door. When he got to the kitchen, Shawn was waiting for him with a huge smile on her face. He asked her what was going on.

"Nothing. It's good to see you so rested." He said that he felt good, too. "I know that I do. I don't think that I had a single dream last night. I was so exhausted. Maybe we should do that more often, doze on the couch before going to bed. I know that I was relaxed enough to sleep like the dead."

"I didn't move, I don't think. And I thought for sure I'd be sore from that, but I feel like I've slept good for the first time in a long time." They'd been running at both ends of the candle or something like that, and he knew that the two of them needed to sit down and chill. "We need a vacation. I think that we all do. I saw Kayce today, and he looked like he was tired, too. I wonder when the last time any of us took any time off since the foundation was opened."

"Someone was talking about a cruise, but I don't know what happened to that. It sounded nice and fun. We should bring it up the next time that we see them. I'm all for it. I could use some downtime after the month that I've had." He knew that she'd had a hard month, what with the loss of her son, Finny. "Hell, at this point, I'd even pay for everyone to go just so we can have some fun for a change. The next time you see one of your brothers, bring it up and see what they have to say about it."

"You do the same with the women. I know you see them more than I do." She said she'd made a note on it on her phone, and that was something that she'd gladly do. "The kids will be coming around soon, and we should do it before anyone announces that they're going to have a baby. I know that Ivy is, and so is Molly, but they're still in the earlier stages of their pregnancies, so it will be a while for them to have them."

When he left for work, he made a note in his phone as well. He thought about reaching out to everyone and asking about it, but he knew that early mornings could be hectic for his family. The only reason that he'd gotten out of the house on time today is because of Shawn. He thought about her son dying, and his heart broke for her.

Finny had been a pompous ass. He had demanded that his mother turn over all her investments to him so that he could keep an eye on them. Among other things, he demanded that they not have any children, as he was her firstborn and everything that she had was his. And he positively hated him. Ethan had done nothing to Shawn but become her mate, and that was what had the man up in arms. Finally, when she kicked him out, changing the locks on the doors so that he couldn't get back into the house, he'd hired three men to beat him so that she'd have to allow him to live with them. And once he had his foot in the door, she wouldn't be able to toss him out again. In the end, though, he was beaten so badly by the men that he'd hired, and he died a few days later from the injuries.

His morning started off on a good note. He was able to look over the surgery list from the day before and thought that things were going well. Approving the surgery schedule for the following week, making allowances for emergency surgeries that might have to be done, he was finished by noon. He still had a long day ahead of him and was glad that he could do things like this to make the hospital run smoothly. Going down to get himself something to eat, he heard from Jack.

"I just heard from one of the patrons of the restaurant that the hospital is closing. I know it's not true, but if rumors get around like that, then the place is going to lose business." He said he'd not heard that and asked for the person's sources. *"He said that he heard it from his daughter, who*

works there. Could be a disgruntled employee who is trying to cause trouble. He wouldn't give me her name, but I found it on the credit card he was using. If I give it to you, you'll be careful with it, won't you?"

"Of course I will. I won't even approach her unless I hear about it from someone else." Jack gave him the name. *"Thanks. I hadn't heard anything like that, and I've been out on the floor for the past hour. No one has approached me about it. Like you said, it's probably someone who isn't happy with their job and is hoping to spread rumors to cause trouble."*

"Yeah, I thought that if anyone would know about it, someone would have said something to you about it. That's the way trouble starts." He agreed with him and asked him about the cruise that they'd been planning. *"I remember someone talking about it, but didn't hear anything else. I would love for us all to get together and do something like that. I can leave here for a couple of weeks, and I doubt that anyone would miss me."* The two of them laughed.

"I'm supposed to ask all of you guys about it, and what is going on with it. Shawn is going to talk to the women. I need to have a vacation. I'm about at my wits' end here running this department. It's all going smoothly right now, but I'm stressed waiting for the other shoe to drop. I'm sure most of us are. I know that Denver is worried that the Fosters are going to pull the funding of the foundation every day." They talked about how much fun it would be to go away, even for a single week. *"We'd all come back*

so rested that we'd not have to have another vacation for another year."

They set up a time for a dinner together and decided that was when they'd bring it up. Both things, as a matter of fact. As soon as he closed the connection, he went in search of the woman who was spreading rumors. He wouldn't approach her about it, but he would look into her file to see if she had a reason for telling lies. Perhaps it was something that she did all the time. He'd find out and take care of it soon.

~*~

Molly loved working the phones at the foundation. She was partnered with Lance today, and he was drawing on a pad of paper things that he wanted to blow in his art studio. She was jealous of how well he could draw, and when she asked him about what he was doing, he explained it to her in great detail so that she could nearly see the finished piece of work when he was finished. Answering the phone when it rang again, she pulled up her list of questions when the person said they needed help.

"I just need about five hundred dollars for my rent this month." She asked where she was from and how many people lived in her home. "Just me. I'm having trouble since my husband of twenty years left me for another woman. He emptied out the bank account of all the money that I'd put in there after working two jobs."

They went through the list of questions, and she was setting up an appointment for her to come and talk to one of the people who worked with others when the woman said no. She wasn't having it. She needed it right now and couldn't wait for a 'committee to get off their asses and decide' her fate.

Lance told her to hang up. When she did, she knew that the next phone call was going to be her again, and Lance answered it. He was a bit more firm with her from the start, and she had to marvel at the way he handled her. In the end, she didn't need the money for anything other than a day at the race tracks, and that was all.

"People hear that we're giving away money and they think that they should get a piece of it. That's why the questions are there so that when it comes right down to it, their true colors come through." She asked him why he didn't just take the call from her. "Because she would have been pissed because she had to call back, and those kinds of calls nearly always show what they really want."

"I will keep that in mind." When the next call came through, she took the questions to the next level. Asking if the man who needed the money could wait for a week. That's how long the process would take when you applied for money. Of course, there was money for emergencies, but nothing much that would cause a person to get a lot of cash right away. She loved what she was doing for the foundation and was thinking that she'd work a couple more days a week at it. Telling Lance, he told her she didn't want to do that.

"You'll get burnt out. And jaded. That's why we only work here a couple of days a week and not all week. Hearing people be negative all the time would wear on you, and that would make you upset. You have to balance out your work and family, or you'll get sick. While you might be immortal, you can still cause damage to your health if you don't take care of yourself." She asked if that had happened to anyone working here. "No. When Brook first came to us about answering the phones, that's what she told us. I don't know that anyone from their foundation ever had it happen to them, but I can see it happening. Some days, while I'm here, all I can think about is going home and never returning. Not to say that there aren't good days too, but it's the bad ones that can make you ill. And the ones that you'll remember too when you go home. That's another thing. Don't take your work home with you. That's family time."

"I did notice that when Kayce works here, he never comes home and tells me about his day. I never understood that until just now. Thanks for telling me." He said it was his pleasure. "You all are so nice. I can't believe that you had the parents that you had. Then I met your grandparents, and I understood. They're about the nicest people I've ever met. And they love you boys so much."

"We love them too. They're not immortal, did you know that? They decided that they've been on this earth for about as long as they want and don't want to hang out anymore. I can understand that. I'm going to miss them when they pass, but I understand what they're saying when they say that they only want to live for as long as they have." She wasn't sure about being immortal either and said as much to Lance. "I've been giving it some thought myself. I don't know that I want to outlive my friends. Maybe once the kids start coming, I'll feel differently, but right now I just want to live my life one day at a time and see where that gets me."

"That's what I keep telling myself. And then I think of being around forever, I wonder how many Tuckers that will be in say a hundred years, when all of us are immortal. That will be a lot of people just hanging around for no other reason other than someone decided that they should be immortal." She thought about something else. "What if my kids don't want it either? Will I have to watch them die when they get older? I don't think I could handle that at all. To watch my children get old and die when I'm going to be around for the rest of the days in my life."

They both talked about immortality between calls. She asked him if he'd talked to anyone else about it, and he said that he'd mentioned it to Georgie. But they didn't have any reason right now to not want it. She asked about his grandparents' dying and how he was going to handle that.

"Not well. They raised us, as you know. My grandparents are all that I know as parents, and I don't know what we would have done without them around when they took us in." He told her how his parents had dropped them off one Thanksgiving and never returned. "They were selfish right up until they were killed by the pride. My mom was even upset about them having ten kids and having to raise them. She said that it wasn't their fault. I don't know whose else it would be but theirs, do you?"

"No. Kayce said that he didn't remember them at all, that he was just a toddler when they were left behind." He said that he was old enough to remember how much he hated them when they'd done that to them. Not to mention the grandparents. "They couldn't have been very young when this happened. I wonder what was on their mind when they were suddenly the parents of all of you. They certainly made it work for you guys."

"They made it so we all got to go to college as well. That couldn't have been easy on them either. But there was always food on the table. Not always meat, but there was plenty to go around." She was glad that she'd gotten to know them and told Lance that. "Yes, I am as well. Hopefully, they'll be around for when the kids start coming, but I don't know. They're well into their nineties now and are starting to look it."

"I love the stories that they tell about you boys growing up. Mostly it's just little bits of trouble that you got into as kids, but they're funny to know that you all were just like every little kid around." He said they had their fair share of cuts and bruises, too. "I bet you did. Then, when Dakota got married, and then the other two, it made it a little bit easier around the household. I think that it's amazing that you all still hang out together. Even the married ones."

"We were all we had. It was hard for a person to go anywhere and not know one or two of us. Even when we had part-time jobs around the town we lived in, we'd see one another." Lance told her how they all took home their paychecks when they were still living at the home and made sure that there was money for fees and such. "Grannie would make sure we had spending money too if we worked, but we were all so happy to have a place to be nightly that we'd hand over our checks without a word. They raised us to be that generous with our money. Like I said, family is all we had back then."

"Now look at you. You all still have each other and so much more. Coming here opened up a whole new life for all of you. One I bet you didn't expect either." Lance said he didn't know what he'd do without Georgie in his life. "I know what you mean.

I love Kayce so much, and I can't believe how much I love just being around him. He's become my best friend, too. Plus all the others in the family, too."

At noon, Lance went to get them lunch. There were always vendor trucks around that they could go to, and today was no different. When he came back with Cubans, a delicious sandwich made with roasted pork, ham, dill pickle, and Swiss cheese, and grilled on a specialized bread, she couldn't believe how good it tasted. When he ate all of his, she gave him what she couldn't eat of hers. They were that good.

By three, they had taken a total of thirty calls each. Most of them were going to have interviews on how they could get help. While a few of them were calls like the one she'd had earlier, just people trying to scam a good charity out of some of their cash. She even had one where a woman wanted to drop off her kids for the day so that she could go to work. She said that's what a charity could do for her today. Of course, they didn't take her up on her fine offer but told her that she could call the health department to see if they could help her out.

"Once, when I was working, I had a woman come to the door to ask about diapers. That's a big thing for them to need. They're so expensive, and when she needed help, as you can imagine, she couldn't wait for a week, as she needed them now. I had her come by, and I gave her what money I had on me. It wasn't much, like thirty dollars. But it was enough with what she had to get some diapers." He smiled at the memory, and she joined him. "I wouldn't have done it if Parker hadn't made it so that no one can enter this building with ill will in their hearts. That sort of made me realize that she did indeed need the money, and I felt good about giving it to her."

"Would you do it again?" He shook his head, and she asked him why. "I mean, it turned out well for you and her. Why don't we have a few bucks around so that we can do that when it's needed?"

"Because word would get out and we'd be bombarded by people every day. Can you imagine giving thirty bucks to every person who had a sad story? I mean, that woman from earlier would have taken it and told all her friends how she's scammed this place. They'd be lined up out the door to get their thirty bucks. I might be jaded, and I probably am, but I've learned that people as a whole are screwed up. A person is all right and will stop to help you if you're injured along the side of the road. But get a group of people together, and they'll pull out their cell phone to record what's happening to you before calling 911." She told him she was sorry that he felt that way. "I am too somedays. That's why I blow glass and make love to my wife. Because I'm afraid of getting so deep into thinking that the world is a terrible place that I'll never come out of it. Today I shouldn't have come in, but I thought working with you would be fun. And it has been, don't get me wrong. But I've had a rough couple of weeks getting work done, and I've been suffering."

"Why don't you go home? I can handle this for the next hour. And if I can't, they'll just have to call back when they don't get me." He asked her if she was sure. "I am. I'm not down in the dumps like you are, so I'm fine. Go ahead and leave, and you'll feel better once you get home with Georgie. Go and have a good day, Lance. You deserve it."

When he finally left, she only had an hour to go. The phone rang about a half dozen times, but she could handle it. After locking up and heading home, she felt better, too. She was going to talk to Kayce about Lance and see if he could not work the phones for a while. He needed a break before it became too much for him.

Chapter 7

William wanted to see his daughter, and she'd better get her ass to see him. There was no reason whatsoever that he should be in prison right now, and they were saying that he was going to have murder charges added to his sentence when he was sentenced, and that wasn't fair either. Things were not going his way, and he couldn't understand what the big deal was. He needed answers, and he was going to by god get them, or he was going to have to hurt someone. Someone finally answered the phone at the police station where he'd been.

"Yes, I want someone there to get in touch with my daughter. Her name is Molly Toby." They said that they didn't do that. "Yes, you do. You've done it for me before. I'm locked up in prison now, and no one is helping me understand what is going on. Even my lazy sons are here, and they don't know what's going on either."

"I can give her a message, but I don't have any way of transferring a call to her if she doesn't want me to." He said that would be fine and told the officer what he wanted. "You want her to come and visit you in prison and to bring money. You didn't say how much money to bring, so am I to assume you want her to bring enough to put in your fund?"

"Yes, that's right. In her brothers' funds, too. A couple of grand each would be enough for starting, and then after the first week, we can see how that goes." The man whistled, and he didn't understand that either. "Just tell her, as her father, I demand that she come and see me, and to bring money. Someone here should know how much it'll cost to have me bailed out of them. That judge did me wrong, and I don't believe that I belong here anymore. These people aren't nice to me."

"They're not nice, or they're not doing what you want them to do? There's a big difference, you understand." He said that he didn't understand anything going on around him. "Just tell me your name and a phone number where she can reach you."

"I'm in prison, there's no number here where she can get in touch with me. And I've tried to get one of the guards to give me their cell phone so that I can call her, but they said that it's against the rules for some reason. How am I supposed to get in touch with her if there are all these rules that I'm supposed to abide by? And tell me this, why is it that I have to share my cell with someone else who isn't as clean as I am? He's nasty, is what he is."

"I don't have anything to do with that. You'll have to take that up with the prison warden." He said they won't let him see him. "I would imagine that he's a busy man, what with running a big prison like he is."

After getting off the phone with the man, his phone call was just cut off because he'd hit his time limit. He went back to his cell. That's why he needed a cell phone so badly. It didn't cut you off in mid-sentence. When he got into his cell, the man he was sharing with was naked, lying on his bunk. It nearly had him running from the room, but all he did was yell for the guards. He wasn't supposed to do that, and he told on him every time.

"It's too hot just sitting in the cell all day. Why don't you take yourself someplace else so that I can have my free time? I ain't bothering you any." He pulled on his dirty underwear when he was told to. "It's not like I'm subjecting you to my fantasies. I'm just naked all the time. Damn bastard."

"I don't care how hot it is in the cell. You'll not be spreading your germs all over the place while you share with me. If this keeps up, you're going to have to find someplace else to bunk. I hate germs of any kind." When he pulled on his pants, he felt marginally better, but the man was repulsive. "When was the last time you had a bath or shower? You smell bad, too. Christ, of all the people that I have to bunk with, why did it have to be you?"

"Just lucky, I guess. Just calm your horses. I'm dressed now. I'm also hot, so it's going to make me smell worse. Not that I care, but you should get yourself some smelly candles from the store so that you can burn them. Maybe you'll burn the place down too while you're at it. Won't that be a hoot?" His roommate, whose name he never remembered, was getting on his last nerve. All he wanted him to do was to clean up after himself, but he thought it was funny to rub things into his face. Christ, he needed to talk to the warden soon, or he was going to be bat shit crazy just trying to keep himself healthy. "You think it's a walk in the park being in here with you all the time? It's not let me tell you."

Going out into the general population again, he didn't think it was any better. There was a man doing his nails right there at the table he'd eaten at last evening. Another man was playing cards with cards so dirty they were black from the user's hands. Sitting at a table close to the guard's station, he was alone there. Someone was going to have to get him his daughter here so that she could get him out of here. She wasn't much good for anything else; she might as well make it so that he could be free of all the people in the prison, at least.

William didn't read the newspaper for anything but to see if anyone he knew had died. He would occasionally look up some arrests that had happened around town, but never saw his name in the paper. That's why he was so confused about the murder thing.

If he was going to be arrested for murdering again, why wasn't his name in the paper? He thought the judge had it all wrong until he got here. Then he heard from several inmates that they were in for their third time murdering someone. He just couldn't believe it.

"Inmate, you have a phone message. It's from your daughter. She said to stop calling her that she likes you right where you are." He asked about bailing him out. "There was no bail set for you, so there is nothing that she can pay to get you out."

"That's not right. I have to have bail. That's the way things work when you're in jail." He pointed out that he wasn't in jail but in prison, and things were different from what they were there. "I don't see why they are. It's the same thing. People are still in cells because they did something wrong. I've done nothing wrong other than have myself a daughter who is as ungrateful as her brothers. At least they could be depended on when I have a job to do. She's worthless." They didn't say anything back to him, so he asked again about using one of their cell phones. They asked if he had her number. "It should be programmed into your phone. It was on mine when I had it. Just look under bitch. That's what I had her named on my phone."

The three men standing there laughed and asked him why that would be in their phone. He explained to them that he'd put it in his phone, and it should be in all cell phones. That's the way things work.

"No, it doesn't. You had your own numbers put into your cell phone, and I have my own. Not that I'm going to let you use my cell phone, but what do you want to call her for? She's made it perfectly clear that she doesn't want to talk to you. You should just leave her alone." He said that she's his daughter, and he demanded things from her that she should be doing. "Obviously not, or she'd be here visiting you right now. I'm thinking that if you keep bothering her, she's going to complain to the right person and get your phone privileges taken away from you for good."

People were always thinking he was stupid. He might mess up once in a while, but he hadn't worked a day in his life and had a good one, too. There was always money around for him to snitch, and he was smart enough to know when to walk away when his guts were telling him to. Yes, sir, people underestimated him all the time, and he was happy for it. It showed him how smart he was when they did that to him.

He had to think of a way to get Molly here so that he could talk to her. He might be pissed off at her, but she was his only hope of getting out of here. Since she was fixing up his house, surely she had money to spare when it came to him. The very least she could do was set him up a fund so that he could bribe the guards into getting him a new cell without anyone to share it with. Then he thought of something else.

"Hey, did I get any mail? I'm supposed to have

my father's checks mailed directly to me. He don't need it anymore because he's in the nursing home. That's another thing that Molly should be doing, paying for him to be there since she put him in there." One of them asked what checks that would be. "His monthly checks. The judge agreed with me about me having them since he was being taken care of, so I should be getting them mailed here. Since he put me here for some reason."

"First of all, no, you don't have any mail. Secondly, his Social Security checks won't come here for you because they're his and not yours. Since you've never worked a day in your life, I would imagine that you don't have anything coming to you. Thirdly, and I can't believe I have to say this to you, this isn't a bank where you can just get checks and have them cashed for you. What good would it do you to have them mailed to you in the first place? Not that I think the judge even said that, but you're not getting them mailed to you anywhere you might be. They don't belong to you." There was just no talking to some people, he thought when he spouted off things that he knew were true. "What person on earth would take their money from their own father and expect to get away with it? No one that I know."

"Shows what you know. People do it all the time. They even get them coming to them when their benefactor dies. I've seen it firsthand." He asked him who it was. He'd like to tell the judge about them. "No, I'm not telling you. That trick was played on me before, and I'm not falling for it again."

"Whatever. Just don't expect the checks to come here for you. They more than likely belong to the nursing home now that he's staying in to offset some of the money required for him to be there." He'd gone over this before and wasn't going to repeat himself. Turning his back to the men standing there, he wondered why they were telling him lies.

The judge had said that he was going to get what was coming to him, and he couldn't think of anything else more important than the money. Unless it was getting out of here, and that was looking slimmer by the day. He'd already been here for two weeks, and no one had come to visit him. Even his sons were avoiding him when he saw them in the general population.

That was another thing that he didn't understand. Why was it called the general population? He knew that everyone who was anyone met in the big common room, but what did it have to do with someone being a general? The only people that seemed to be in charge were the guards, and they didn't look like they were in charge of much. Everyone just walked around talking to one another or playing games.

He wanted to know, but not enough to talk to the guards again. They didn't seem to know all that much, and he wasn't going to engage with them again if he could help it. Hopefully, he'd get his checks soon, and they'd tell him about them. He wondered if they could hold them for some reason, and that would not be right. He needed that money so that he could have the extras like the rest of the people here did. He didn't know what it would be, but he knew from the last time he'd been in prison that it could buy you a lot of shit that you could trade with. He laid his head down on the table when he was feeling exhausted again.

He had not been sleeping well since he'd been in this place. There was just too much noise going on during the nighttime hours that he would wake up every time he heard something. He was used to having a dark room when he was sleeping, so that wasn't a problem; it was just the noise. One of them being that his roommate snored loudly and farted in his sleep. Sometimes the smell would be so bad that he'd gag.

The man was a pig, and anyone who would have to spend about ten minutes with him would know it. He wanted a different person to share his room with, or none at all. That would suit him just fine if he had a cell all to his own. That was another thing that Molly could make happen for him, and that was paying for him to have his own room. She was slacking on her duties to him, and he was starting to get pissed off about her.

When dinner was called, someone shook him awake. He did feel better after his nap and was glad to be able to stretch out when he wanted. He was getting too old to be sleeping like he'd been and his body was telling him in creaking up. When he stretched his arms up and over his head, he felt something in his back pull, and it made him sick, it was so painful.

"You all right, inmate?" He said that his name was William Toby. "You're just another inmate to me. What's wrong with you?"

"I pulled something in my back, and it hurts." The guard asked if he needed medical assistance, and he said he'd be all right. "I can handle a few aches and pains. I'm just old, that's all." If he expected someone to tell him he was in the prime of his life, he was disappointed. People were just rude anymore, and he couldn't stand to be around them. As soon as he had his tray, he thought of another thing that Molly should be doing for him. Getting him some meals that didn't look like they had been made by a deranged person. All his food was touching, and he couldn't stand that.

~*~

Kayce had two assistants working for him now. One of them was a nurse, the other was going to be his receptionist. He liked having just one or two people to work with, and he thought that they could get along well. His office was now ready for patients, and he was happy to see that they were using them as their doctor.

After seeing the infant, who was an hour old, he declared her healthy and made sure that her blood work was taken so that she could be released. He'd see her again in a couple of weeks, and he was well on his way to having patients of his own. He still helped out with the family, but he was all right with his own practice. Kayce had the best job in the world, he thought. Taking care of children.

After seeing one of his patients from the old place, he was ready to go home. But just as he was leaving, he was paged over the intercom system. Unsure what was going on, he made his way to the nurses' station and picked up the phone. It was his brother Colby.

"I have a slight issue. One of the men on my route out has hooked himself with a fishing hook. What can I do to keep him from getting an infection while I bring him onto shore? I don't know how he did it, other than he was fucking around and got it hooked into his wrist." He asked where it was on his wrist. "I'll send you a picture. I thought you might ask me that."

When he received the picture, he told his brother to put his hand in ice and to get him to shore as soon as possible. It looked to him like it was close to the artery, and he didn't want to take any chances of the man bleeding out before he could get a look at him.

"I'll call you an ambulance to be where you dock as soon as I get off the phone with you. It might not be much, but I'd rather not take the chance like you said." He thanked him. "Does this sort of thing happen much? I never thought that someone who would be out on the boat would be hurt. I guess I wasn't thinking about all the things that could go wrong."

"I've never had it happen before either. But like I said, he was fucking around, and he got himself hurt. The others with him are pissed off at him. Thankfully, not at me, but enough where they're telling him that they're not going to go to the hospital with him. They want to go back out to sea, and I'm going to take them." Kayce asked him if he had a good first aid kit on board. "I do. I went top of the line with it so that if something came up, I'd be able to take care of it. But believe it or not, there isn't any kind of shit in it for stupidity." The two of them laughed hard about that.

"I'll have the emergency room ready for him when they get here. I'm trying hard not to take any adults on but family. He'll more than likely have his own doctor to look at it when they get him finished up here." He said that he was calling his doctor now, and he should be there for him when he arrived. "That's good. That way, he can tell him what an idiot he'd been in fucking around on a ship out to sea."

"I know, right? When I get him dropped off, I'm going to have to clean the ship where he bled all over the place. He's acting like it's no big deal, so I have to wonder if he's like this all the time. A showoff to his buddies. They seemed to be resigned to the fact that he'd been hurt." He asked how many were on the boat with him. "Three, counting the man who is hurt. We should be on shore in about ten minutes. Give or take a couple. I can see the ambulance there now. Good job on getting them called."

"I had a nurse do it for you. She said that she's always wanted to go deep-sea fishing, so I told her about your business." He thanked him again. "No worries. It's the least I can do for you making work for the hospital." When Kayce said he had to go, he put the phone on the receiver. Thanking the nurse for her help, she waved him off like it was an everyday thing to have to call an ambulance for a ship-to-shore kind of thing.

Going back to his office—he loved saying that—he filled out the paperwork on the newborn. Making a file for her, he put it with the other dozen or so new files that he'd made since opening up. Just as he was ready to go home for the day, Margaret came into his office and sat down. He watched her to see what was going on.

"We might have a problem in the lobby." He nodded, waiting for more information. "You're a lion, right? I mean, I should probably know that, but I'm making sure. You are a shifter anyway, right?"

"I'm a lion. What's going on in the lobby that has you freaked out?" She told him. "So you don't believe that he fell down and hurt himself. Has this person been in the offices before? I don't mean here, but where you worked before?"

"He brought the little girl in mostly to the emergency room, but they were making noises of calling the police, and now he's going to all the offices around town. You just happen to be new, and I'm thinking that he's going to be hoping that you're stupid." She asked him if he was understanding what she was saying.

"Yes. You believe that he's abusing the little girl and hopes that I won't notice any other wounds on her body. I'm assuming that there are." She nodded. "All right. Set them up in one of the rooms, and I'll go see her. Do you know how she's injured this time?"

"It looks like her ankle might be broken, and she has a split lip, too. It's going to need stitches if I don't miss my bet. I can get a tray ready for her when you see her." He stood up when she did. "Be careful. He's been known to take his frustrations out on whoever tells him that she's been hurt by other means. I'm not saying you can't handle yourself, but just be careful when you get him in the room with you."

As soon as he was in the room with the man and the little girl, he could smell her pain. It wasn't something that he could normally do, but it was as if he was tasting her pain through his body. As soon as he had a look at her ankle, he knew she was going to need to be casted. Telling the man that he had to x-ray her ankle for him to be sure, he started yelling about the cost.

"I don't know what insurance you have, but I'm sure they'll pay for her to have x-rays of her foot and ankle. It might need surgery, too." He said that he didn't have any insurance as they had dropped him for having so many claims. "Does she fall a great deal? Perhaps I should check her ears out, too. She might have something wrong with her inner ear that is causing her to fall a great deal."

"You're just wanting to jack up her bill now that you've got her in here. Just wrap her up and send her home with me. I'll make sure she gets what she needs." He wasn't going to allow this child to go anywhere near that man if he could help it. "You got one of those ace bandages that you can take care of her with, don't you?"

"As I said, I believe it's broken, and I can't wrap it up with a bandage without making sure. As you said, it might only need that, but I need to make sure. It's the law." He bristled when he mentioned the law and said that he didn't have to call the police. "All right. I'll have her x-rayed, and we'll go from there. It won't take but a few minutes, and you can wait right here."

"I'm going with her." He said that the room they did those in was too small for that many people he was going to have to wait. "You just leave the door open for me, and I'll stand outside."

"That won't work either, as it needs to be dark in the room. One would think that you're afraid of leaving her alone with me. Is that the case?" He said that she was his little girl and he wanted her to be safe. "Then let me check her ears too to make sure that she's not having an infection needlessly."

As soon as he stood up to take the girl, the man grabbed his arm. It was all he could do not to shift and take his throat out. Asking him to unhand him got him nowhere, and when he removed his hand from him physically, the man drew back and punched him in the face. That was all it took for his lion to make himself known to the man.

"Parker, I have a problem." Not only was the little girl cringing from him on the examining table, but she was screaming too. Not that he blamed her, he'd just killed her father, and there was blood everywhere. *"I've just killed a man with a witness."*

"I'm coming." She appeared in the room in seconds, which didn't help the situation with the daughter. Touching her fingers to her head, she laid down on the bed and closed her eyes. She was either sleeping or Parker had killed her. Right now, he didn't know what to think. "He's dead all right. You did good. He's been abusing this little girl since he stole her from her mom. She's dead too, but I didn't kill anyone. Thank you for thinking that I have it in me to do that."

"I don't know what you're going to do to help me out, but when we had a situation like this one, we're supposed to call you." He looked at the man with his throat gone and wondered what he was going to do about being in prison for the rest of his life. "What can you do to help me? He hit me, and that's why I reacted the way that I did."

"It'll look like he killed himself when the police arrive. Where's Margaret?" He wasn't sure when she found out his nurse's name, but told her. "She'll take the little girl down to X-ray, and you'll be in your office. You heard what you thought was a gunshot sound, and that's when you found him. All right?"

"This in no way looks like he killed himself." She told him to trust her. "I do. Right now with my life. Molly is going to have a baby, and I'd like to be on this side of the bars to hold it when it comes."

"Call the police, Kayce. It'll be fine, I promise." He hoped so. Going to his office, he made the call about a man who had died in his office. The police asked him for his name, and he told them. They meant the victim.

"Sorry. I didn't get it. I was more concerned with his daughter being hurt the way that she was. Her ankle is broken, I'm sure, but she's covered in bruises all over her body." He asked if his name was Sheppard. "I don't know, but if that's the first name that pops into your head, then it's more than likely him. He's been abusing his daughter, I believe."

"It's him then. We're sending a car over there now. Don't touch anything." He said that he'd not and would wait for him. "I hope he killed himself. It would make that little girl of his life so much better."

When they arrived, he did nothing but show them into the room. Margaret was still in the x-ray with Elizabeth, the little girl, and the officers said it looked like he'd killed himself. Parker had left him there, and he thanked her through their link. She laughed and told him that she had his back, and he hoped so. He didn't like to think about what would have happened had she not been there for him when he needed her.

"Elizabeth won't remember a thing that happened to her dad. She'll just have a fuzzy memory of you taking her back to get films made of her ankle, and that's because she was in so much pain. He knocked her around with a golf club when she didn't make him any dinner. She's not eaten for several days, you're going to find out and admit her. She's going to need someone to come and get her, and I'll have the numbers for you in a little while. She has an aunt and uncle who will take her in with them." He asked her if she was sure that he wasn't going to be in trouble. *"You're going to be fine. You took a bad guy out, and the world will be a better place for it. Don't forget to tell Margaret thanks for the heads up. She more than likely saved you from a good beating."*

The police had him call his one patient and let them know that an emergency had come up and that the offices were closed for the day. It would take him that long to get the mess cleaned up, but Parker told him she'd take care of it. He was so thankful that she was on his side. He hated to think what would have happened had she turned him down with her help. He'd surely be in prison right now.

Chapter 8

Thirteen years later

Denver looked at the work he'd gotten done today and was proud of himself. It had been a few days since he'd had time to play out in his building, and he thought that it was the best thing to relax with. As he was putting the pot he'd just thrown on the cart, he saw Bailee standing in the doorway watching him.

"I have seen you do that a million times, and it never gets old." He thanked her. "No problem. I was wondering what you wanted to do about dinner. I'm hungry and need something to eat soon, or I'm going to expire. How about I order some Chinese and we pig out on that? I want a gallon of hot sour soup."

"That sounds wonderful. Don't forget tomorrow night, I'm having dinner with my brothers. I guess you have that thing with the women, too." She said they were meeting at their home so that they could pig out on food there. "Good. I know that Sally June, our cook, has been getting with you about little sandwiches."

"We're going to be trying out some of the recipes from Jack's old place. He handed over the ingredients list to me the other day. Do you suppose that he'll ever open another place like that one? It's difficult to get into the place now that he has people working for him all the time. I'm betting the family table is used nightly by other patrons." Denver said he thought he was having a good time working with their sister in the catering business to care. "I thought about using them to come to the house, but they're booked up again through the rest of the year. Can you imagine having so much business that you don't have any openings for nearly a year?"

"I have orders that need to go out soon, so I can get an idea. I'm ready to quit here. If you want to order, I'll be inside in a minute. I need to clean up and cover things up." She said that she'd do that and went out the door. After finishing the pot that he was working on, he put it on the shelf with the others and began cleaning himself up. He wasn't a messy potter; he'd been doing it for so long, but sometimes he'd get really splashed with some of the mud that he used, so he'd need to change his clothing when he was finished.

After wrapping his work in plastic around the cart, he made sure that everything was put away. He didn't want to leave things out to dry out too quickly and turned off the lights when all was cleaned up. As soon as he was in the house, he washed up again and decided he wasn't too dirty, but for his shirt. Taking it off near the washer, he dropped it into it and got himself a clean one. It was nice to be able to have a clean shirt on this level when he needed it.

The food arrived just as he was setting the table in the dining room. She must have ordered one of everything on the menu because he couldn't believe how much food there was for the two of them. The kids had already eaten, she told him, and were off playing in their rooms. He was glad that he didn't miss bedtime again. It was his favorite part of the evening, reading to the three of them.

He loved his children as much as he did Bailee. He had two sons and a daughter, whom he thought the world set in her heart just for him. Lee would smile at him, and he'd feel the earth shift under his feet. The boys loved her too, as she was their little sister and they spoiled her rotten. But she knew when she was in trouble at home and had to stand in the corner. He'd never tell her this, but when he'd been small, he'd spent a great deal of time standing in one corner or another in Grannie's home.

Just as they were finishing up their meal, the kids came down to tell him goodnight. They'd had their baths already and smelled so good that he found himself sniffing their throats for the scent. It also smelled of their mother, so he was happy to know that they smelled of her as well. Denver got to take them up to bed while Bailee cleaned up. She said it was because he'd missed bathtime, but he had a feeling that she knew what it meant to him to be able to read to them.

It made his night.

Settling down on Harmans bed, his oldest, he asked him where they were in the book they'd been reading. He'd been reading the one about the whale, and they were about halfway through it now. He started on the chapter that they'd left off on when Lee, his second-oldest son, asked him a question about being a lion alpha.

"It's called leap leader, and it's different for everyone who does it. I set up hours to work so that I didn't have people coming and going all the time. It afforded me time to be with your mom, too. You know how much we love to spend time together." They all three made the gagging sounds, and he laughed. "Being in charge is a big deal. You have to know all the rules that govern everyone and be willing to make sure justice is served when it needs to be. It's a big responsibility just being the leader of this family."

"Do you suppose I can run the pride when I'm older? I'm learning all the rules so that I don't mess up. I'd love to be able to rule people all the time." He simply nodded, knowing that for a ten-year-old, he had no idea what it was like to rule. "I'd make everyone bow down before me like we read about in that one book. I would make sure, too, that I had people around me who would do what I said to them, no matter what it was."

"I'm sure you're thinking that's a good thing,

but would you want the family to hate you?" He shook his head no and said they'd love him. "Only if you're fair. And to me, it sounds like you only want things for yourself. That's what is important when running a pride: you have to be fair about everything you do. It might mean that you have to tell them no once in a while, but it's for the good of everyone, not just for yourself. Understand?"

"Yes. But I'd still like them to bow down to me like they do Uncle Ronin. Everybody about kills themselves getting to the ground when he comes around." He told him because he was king of their kind. "Then that's what I want to be someday. King of all lions. Wouldn't that be so cool, Amy?"

"You'd just be a wiener head, and you know it. You don't have good enough grades to run anything." He had to stifle a laugh when she played the grade card. "If you were to just do the homework, then you'd be able to have good grades like Lee and I. But you have to show off, don't you?"

And then there was a fight. After letting them wrestle for a little while, he broke it up. Amy was winning anyway, as they knew better than to hit her first. They could defend themselves against her, but seeing that she was smaller than them and a girl, they would cut her some slack. After settling down again, he read a chapter to them and told them it was bedtime. Each of them had their own room, so he got to go from room to room kissing them goodnight. He stayed a little longer in Harmon's room because he had more questions.

"Do you think I'll have a mate, Dad?" He told him that he didn't know why not. he was a lion after all. "I don't know that I want one. If they have to be a girl like Amy is, she'll drive me crazy all the time about rules. I know the rules, I just don't have to like them."

"You'll get used to them. And when she comes around, you'll be happy that she found you. I know for a fact that I was when your mom found me." He asked if they'd have to do kissing and stuff. "I should hope so. But you'll be older then and won't mind it so much. So long as you remember the most important rule of all."

"It's her body and her right. I remember that one. When a woman says no, they mean it too." When he had him tucked in, he kissed him on the forehead. "I don't mind when mommy kisses me, Dad, but I love it when you kiss my forehead. I feel like a grown-up little boy."

"Good, I'll remember that from now on so that I don't kiss you on the cheek." After turning off the light, he told his son good night. All he could think about was his brother Lance and him not wanting a mate either before meeting Georgie. He nearly lost her when he started spouting off the crap that he'd been.

"Did you get them all to bed? I swear to you,

Harmon asks about two million questions a day. I bet you that he makes a list in his head while he's sleeping, and that's why they come out during the day." He told her about the mate question. "I hope you reminded him that it doesn't matter if he wants her or not, she's his forever."

"If I told him that, he'd never leave the house for fear of finding her." The two of them laughed and sat down on the couch together. "He wants to be king someday because he wants people to bow before him. I didn't tell him that we need to bow before Ronin, but he's a bit young for that kind of advice. I'll save that for when he's older, and it means something to him about Ronin."

"Have you spoken to the others about what we were talking about yesterday?" He said that he'd not but would at the Friday meeting. They'd been getting together on Friday nights for the past ten years. It had worked out well for them. "I've been talking to the girls. They'll have an opinion when the time is right. I don't think that any of us wants to be immortal anymore. I know that I've given it a great deal of thought, and I just want to die like your grandparents did. In each other's arms while slipping away in their sleep. That's so romantic."

"The fact that they knew it was time to go boggled my mind. Grannie had us all over for dinner and told us that they were going to go home. Imagine my surprise when they didn't mean Texas." She said she didn't think that any of them got it until Lance did. "No, he understood before any of us. I'm glad too. I felt foolish for thinking what I did. And then within three days they were both gone."

He missed them every day. There wasn't a day that went by that he didn't think of them and miss them. When he remembered that they'd died, he'd get sad again and miss them all more. They'd been a huge part of their lives, and now that they were gone, he realized how much more they'd done for them when they'd been alive.

"I've been thinking about something else when I was cleaning up the dining room. I think I'd like to have another baby." He said he was game if she was. "Just like that? You're willing to have another child because I want one?"

"I would do anything for you. And that includes having another child if you want to." She told him that she did and was wondering when they could start on it. He told her right now, and she laughed at him. "How about I lock up the house, and we go up to our bedroom and try? You're not ovulating right now, but that doesn't mean we can practice. You remember how much practicing we did before Amy came along, don't you?"

"I'm surprised that she wasn't twins or more, the way that we kept at it." She kissed him on the mouth, and he held her to him. "I love you, Denver Tucker. With all that I am."

"And I love you too, my dearest heart. You make me a better man when you're around, and I couldn't be happier with the results." After standing up, Bailee went off to bed. He locked up the house and turned off the lights.

He loved this old house and thought that it was the perfect size to have more children in. He couldn't wait to tell his family that they were trying again and would be thrilled if they had another girl. Just so long as it was healthy, he really didn't care what it was.

After getting up to the bedroom, he locked their doors too. The kids knew that they locked the door at night and would know to pound on the door if they needed them. Harmon had nearly walked in on them when he'd just been a little boy so they started locking their door nightly. He didn't want to scar his children for the rest of their lives by them walking in on them when they were making love. It was a habit that he thought all his brothers had since they all had kids. No matter how little they were, things had a way of just coming up when they were around.

~*~

Lance put the glass bowl in the hot kiln so that it wouldn't cool off too quickly. He'd been making a set of stacking bowls for the last few days, and he thought he was finally getting the hang of it. The trouble was, he was having a hard time not making them all big. But Ivy told him that she needed a set for serving at the table, and he was going to get them even if he had to use all the glass in his shop. Not that he thought that was possible. He had a seemingly endless supply of glass that he worked with.

"I have an order for you." He looked up at David, his brother-in-law, when he came into the room. "Can I help you with that? I've gotten pretty good at cutting for you when I just show up."

"I just have to set it on the mold. If you could just give me a few minutes, I'll have it there, and we can talk." He said he'd stand out of the way. "Thanks. It's dangerous being out here when I'm blowing."

The mold took the glass like he wanted, and he moved it around so that it would be even. Picking the mold and glass up, he headed for the kiln again and put the two pieces in it to cool down. He even loved the colors of this set that he was making. The dark green was going to look good in Ivy's home, too. He looked at David when he was finished.

"That amazes me every time I see you do it. I would fumble and fall with it when I tried to move it to where he needed to be." Lance told him that he'd done that several times, and it never got any easier. "I bet not. About this order. I think you'll understand what we need. I need at least a dozen little bowls about the same size. We want to put herbs in them as we use them, so that they don't get all mixed up at the same time. I think that Dakota called them pinch pots. Just big enough to take a pinch out of them to put into whatever we're cooking."

"I have a set of those already." He went across the room and pulled the large box of glassware off the shelf. "I was trying to figure out if I could get the same sizes made up when I was working the other week. I thought that I'd put them in the shop as pinch pots, good name for them by the way, and see if I could get rid of them that way. Take what you want of them or all of them if they'll work for you."

"These are perfect. And I love the colors too. Where did you get this bright red from? I think that's the most beautiful color I've seen you use out here." He said he'd been mixing broken glass with some of the colored glass that he had, and it came out that way. "Which means you'll never get the color again. I remember you telling me that once. How you had this blue color that you dearly loved and couldn't get it again."

"That's right. I remember telling you that." David was going through the box and stacking them on the table in size. "How are those going to work for what you had in mind? I don't mind making you something different if they're too small."

"They're perfect. And I love that I have so many of them. Are you sure you don't want to sell them sometime? I mean, there must be about three dozen of them." He said he was just going to put a couple of bucks on them when he sold them, and he was doing him a favor by taking them all. "If you're sure, I'll take them. This is going to save us a lot of time in prep work. I'm going to have to label them, but I'm thinking now that they're in colors, we can just remember the colors. I love them."

After David left him in order to take the cups to his wife, Lance started breaking up glass for the next project he had in mind. He'd been thinking about it for the last week and thought that he had all the processes down in the way that he needed them to be made. Just as he was cleaning up his mess, Adonna, the queen of the fae, appeared in his building.

"I waited to see what you'd be doing next when I wanted to come here. I have some news for you. The little birdbaths that you made for my people have become a good hit. I've been using them for special awards when they do something extraordinary. They really love them." He said he was glad, and like he did for his brother, he went over to his shelf and pulled down the box of them he had. "Oh, how beautiful. These will be perfect for the next round of giveaways. You're so talented, can't you tell me something that you want so that I can repay you for it? You've made so many of them now, I'm sure that everyone will have one by the end of the next sowing season."

"Just pay it forward like you're forever telling me to do." She flushed brightly, and he had to smile. He'd made an ancient woman blush, and he felt good about that. "You could do me a favor, though. Not that you'd have to do it, but the next time you're playing around with the roses at my grannie's house, could you please make it so that all of us can have a bush started from them? You don't have to do it if it puts you behind. I know you're on a tight schedule as it is."

"I would love to do that for the family. I'll have them finished up in a week. That way, I can make sure that the seedlings are going to be strong enough to hold their shape. Your grannie had the most beautiful flowers of all the gardens around her. She loved them so, and I can understand why you want a cutting for yourself." He said that he wasn't going to tell his family until he had them, so they'd be surprised. "What a wonderful thought. Yes, I'll be very careful about not telling them about them, too. You have a brilliant mind, and I so love you."

"I love you too, my lady. You and I have gotten along so well over the seasons that I feel like we're related on some level." She flushed again, and he had to laugh. "When you get them, let me know. I've already got the little containers made up for them. It's pieces of the glasses that we used when we would all go over there."

"They'll treasure it all from you." When she

left him, telling him that she might need more of them sometime soon, he decided to make a list of things that he was going to need to get her an order done.

They were so tiny that he could produce them in about a week, but it was getting them to set up that took him the longest. He loved playing around with the sets of them just because they were so small. And he loved the colors that he used too. When he had a bit left over from a project, he would make a couple of the bowls or stands, and that was what got them done so quickly.

Working on his project again, he heard from the house. Dinner would be soon, and he needed to get to a point where he could stop. He would do that because if he got caught up in something, he'd never make it out of here, and dinner would be ruined. His kids would later come out and get him, and he was worried that they'd get hurt. It was a place that was too hot for kids to be running around. While he was between projects, he made his way into the house.

"I have some things that I need to run by you, too. It has to do with the foundation. Did you know that Denver hired ten new people to answer the phones?" He said that he'd helped interview them. "Good. I was hoping that was the case. I have to work with one of them tomorrow. Is there anything I need to know about the lot of them? I mean, are they going to be a bunch of teeny boppers or something?"

"No, they're from the assisted living home where William used to stay. They just want to work about ten hours a week, and since we can have them come in a day at a time and work the phones, it's no hardship for us to accommodate them." She asked why he'd hired so many. "I think he was thinking that they all might not work out, and he wanted to get them trained before we all took our cruise again."

"That's right. The first and second week of October. I'm looking forward to that a lot. Are you?" He said that he'd not given it much thought as he'd been really busy out in the barn. "I know you have. And I saw the cups you gave David. They'll be perfect for what they have in mind for them. Also, did you notice that he shaved off his beard again? That usually means that they're going to have another baby. I'm happy with the four that we have right now. Maybe later we can talk about having another one, but for now, four is just enough."

"I agree. But if you want another, all you have to say is you're ready, and I'll be there for you." She laughed, telling him that he just wanted to make the baby. "Of course I do. That's most of my fun. You do all the hard work while I just sit back and bask in the fact that I've created a child with the only woman that I'll ever love."

"You're so sappy." She kissed him then, and he took the plates from her to set the table. He'd made them, he knew and loved the way that his family used them for everyday uses. He wondered if his family used theirs as much as he did. "Don't forget we have Toby staying the night with us. He's here until Saturday. Then his mom is going to pick him up, and we're headed to the auction."

Georgie had a successful décor business. She would go into a home and make it shine again. The stuff that she picked up at auctions would be put to good use, and he couldn't believe some of the prices that she paid for things. He had to let her go through his glass that he could buy at nearly every one of the auctions, so that if she found a piece that she thought she could use, he'd not break it up for projects. It was fun for him to do that for her, and she seemed to have a good time going to auctions, too.

Dinner was tacos, and he loved them. Georgie thought that the kids would be messy when they ate them, and they were. But clean up was easy, as he'd been getting used to having to sweep up cheese and tacos from the floor. When she cooked, he cleaned up the mess. They didn't leave that for the staff to clean up; it wasn't right that they had to do that.

After getting the kids to bed, Toby sleeping in the boys' room with them, he read to his daughters and put them to bed. He knew they'd be up in a few minutes; there was someone new in the house, but he couldn't begrudge them a little time playing around when he knew that's what he'd done as a child, too. He thought about his parents then and wondered where that thought had come from. It's not like they had much to do with his childhood, and even that had been horrific, but think about them, he did. he wondered what they'd think about all of them having kids.

Probably run screaming from the room. They had hated them that much; he didn't think they'd treat their grandkids any differently. He remembered a time when he'd asked for someone to spend the night with them and was told that he'd have to give them his portion of food. That's why he encouraged his own kids to have someone over because he'd missed that growing up. Grannie would have allowed it, but there had been so much going on around the house back then that he'd been afraid that someone would get lost in the shuffle. He also knew that she'd put an extra plate on the table even if they didn't have that much and feed them as well as she had them. Grannie and Grandda had been gone for nearly twelve years now, and he missed them all the time.

"Did you hear about the immortality things that are going on?" Lance asked Georgie what she meant. "We're not the only ones who have decided not to have it anymore. I guess your entire family is all for just dying when it's their time."

"I'd heard that Denver and Colby had decided that, but I'd had no idea that the rest of them had too. Good for them. I wouldn't want to be the last man standing when we all get to that age. I think that it would break my heart to have to bury one of my family members and know that I'm going to be around forever, especially with our kids. I would hate for something to happen to them, and I'd have to bury one of them. No thanks."

They continued to talk about it as they made their way up to bed. They'd made their decision right after Grannie and Grandda had died. He didn't feel bad about it either. And when Parker had taken it away, she hugged them, telling them that they were going to have a long and happy life together. He hoped so. He loved his family a great deal and didn't want to lose them anytime soon.

Once Georgie was asleep, he got out of bed and went down to his barn. He would do that a couple of nights a week, just so he could get lost in the art of what he was doing. As soon as he had things set up the way that he wanted, he worked on the large bowl that Jack wanted. It wanted to be able to mix coleslaw in it and not have to dirty three bowls to have enough. He thought that the bowl was going to be too heavy for a mixing bowl, but he'd do just about anything for his family. Even if he had to work all night.

Chapter 9

Taking notes as he usually did, Ethan wondered how the other people in the room remembered in detail anything that was being said. None of them took notes. One of them was even playing on his phone under the table. If he could see him, he was sure that the director of the hospital could as well. Maybe they didn't care what happened in their departments?

After the meeting, he waited around to talk to Mr. Humphrey. He'd been new to the role of hospital president and wanted to get his take on the things that he'd seen so far. But he rushed out of the meeting so quickly that he barely got in a hello before he was gone. He did end up talking to the director, Mrs. Challenger. He had a couple of questions for her.

"Who was that man playing on his phone?" He said his name before he could think that he should have kept his mouth shut. "I don't know why they don't allow me to take phones from people when I have a meeting. They're a distraction, and I don't care for them. I suppose they have their functions, but for the life of me, I don't know what it would be in a departmental meeting. What can I do for you, Ethan?"

"You mentioned that there were going to be

cutbacks in certain departments. I'd like a heads up if it's going to be in mine. I have everyone working now, and it would be a shame to have to redo the schedule again." He smiled at her when she smiled at him. It was a creepy smile she gave him, and he took a step back. "Is everything all right?"

"I only said that to see who was paying attention." He didn't like that but kept his mouth shut. I suppose I should have figured that you'd be the only one. You're the only one that pays attention in my meetings, and I couldn't love you more for that."

"Yes, well…" He felt uncomfortable with her words of love and took another step back from her. "I do the best that I can with what I have before me. Also, before I forget, remember that I take the first two weeks off in October again. We get together as a family yearly to celebrate life."

"I have it on my calendar. Don't you have like, a really large family that you get together with? That must be difficult for you. All those people that you're related to at one time. If you really don't want to go I can fix it so that you don't have to. I could accidentally schedule you to work and get you out of it all." He said no, that he loved it. "I can't imagine getting with my family on purpose every year. The things that I could tell you would make your hair turn white. We can barely stand each other when there's a funeral going on, I can't think that getting together would be all that fun that I'd plan."

"It's the only time we can get together without work involved. We all work hard throughout the year so that we can get together for these two weeks. We even take all the kids with us when we go." She pretended to faint, and he didn't know what he was supposed to do. "If you could just make sure that I have the time off, I'd appreciate it. I put it in about a month ago, and it's been approved by my department."

"Yes, so I see. Well, if you change your mind, let me know. I could certainly use you around here when things are going to shit." He wanted to be away from her now and couldn't think of a single reason to leave. Just turning on his heel and leaving, she called him back for a second, she said, and he went back reluctantly. "Next month I'll be job shadowing you, don't forget. It's the highlight of my year getting to follow you around for the day. You do such a good job that I want to do it daily just to be in your presence."

Moving away from her, he decided that he needed to talk to Shawn. What he really needed to do was to hold her. He felt dirty talking to Mrs. Challenger and wanted his wife around so that he could tell her what happened and see if it was just him. It felt like she was coming onto him, and he didn't know what to do.

"Tell her to back the fuck off, you belong to me." He said what if he'd been wrong about what she'd said. "If she's made you feel uncomfortable, then you're not wrong. She was coming onto you. She's in a position of authority over you and is making lewd comments. I don't like that she's thinking that you don't want to go on the cruise in October. That sort of pisses me off."

"I'm just going to avoid her from now on. I wish you were here with me. I could use some of your magical hugs." He'd been calling them that since they started seeing one another. "Remember the first time we were together? You and I were having lunch at your dining room table when you told me to move in with you."

"I remember. It was to piss off Finn." Yes, there was that. Her son had caused trouble for the three of them for months before he was killed one evening. He'd hired men to beat him up, and they'd done such a good job at it that he died from his injuries a few days later. "There are times when I miss him. But we have Finny here. Did I tell you that he's remembered more treasures around the place? We'll dig them up this weekend when you're off."

"All right. I'd love that." He tried to put the lewd comments out of his mind and concentrate on his wife. She was the world to him, as were their children. "Are we taking the kids with us this time? They sort of got out of hand the last time we took them treasure hunting."

He laughed at the memory. What they'd done was found a muddy spring and had jumped in it until they were dirty with mud all over them. It took them three baths before they were clean, and the clothing had to be thrown away, it was so caked with the stuff. Even their shoes couldn't have been saved, they were so bad. He had loved every second of it, and so had Shawn. The kids thought they might be in trouble, but in reality, he wanted to join them.

He felt a good deal better when he got off the phone with his wife. They were going out to dinner tonight to celebrate one of his daughters getting on the cheer team, and he was thrilled that she'd been able to do it. They'd have a little more running around to do, taking her to practice and games, but they'd love it because she was doing something that she loved. They had five kids, and he couldn't love them anymore.

Treasure hunting was something that they did as a family, and he loved the antics that the kids got in. With three girls and two boys, he thought he'd be having more dolls around than anything else, but they were just like their mom, into everything around and learning a great deal from it. He was so proud of his family that he wanted to take out billboards to proclaim that he had the best there was. But it would just make his brothers jealous, and that wasn't good. There wouldn't be a billboard left around town that had anything but the best kids on it.

After getting off the phone with Shawn, he did feel a little better. He decided that he was going to avoid Mrs. Challenger for the rest of the day and see if it had been him or her when she'd made him feel dirty. He'd never felt like that before, and it really had made him feel like he needed a shower. He wondered how women felt when the same thing happened to them.

Going down to lunch, he was glad to see his brother Jack. He was picking up the donations that the hospital had given for the next Power Dinner. It was a dinner where all the heads of departments got together and had some fun. He'd never gone and wasn't planning on going this year either. But he did get to hear about it from his family. Jack and Dakota would cater the meal yearly, and he'd get the first-hand scoop about everyone who went.

"Are you planning on going this year?" He said that he wasn't, one of his kids had a recital that night. "You don't even know when it is, do you?" The two of them laughed.

"It's sometime next month. But I'm not going. They usually try to make me come to it, but I have better things to do than be at an open bar kind of thing when there are those around that can't hold their liquor and keep their mouth shut, too." He asked if he was talking about last year. "Yes. Last year, the department head of nursing made a fool of herself by telling people about her nursing staff. Some of those stories were private, and I'm betting if they knew that she told the stories, she'd be in trouble with them all."

"The bar is cash only this year, and I would imagine the reason why is that so many of them got nasty drunk. They had to call cars in to take them home when they got out of hand. I don't even want to go, and I'm part of the food." He said that he was sorry for that. "Not as much as we are. David had to be a bouncer a couple of times, and I know that he didn't care for being the heavy in those circumstances." He said he knew that he'd not enjoy it. "You should come and stay sober and watch them. Even your department head is something of a lush."

"No thanks. I have better things to do." They talked about the food that was going to be at the Power Dinner, and Ethan was impressed. It sounded to him like the hospital was going all out on the food because the bar wasn't going to be open. No one in his family drank; it took a great deal for them to get even a buzz off alcohol, so they didn't bother with it at all. Same with over-the-counter drugs.

"I've been thinking about our vacation a great deal lately." He said that he has the days counted down on his phone. "I believe Shawn does as well. She said it's her one chance to be herself, and she's not giving it up for anything. I didn't know she was holding back on things around the place. She said it was her magic. She can use it when we're all together, and no one cares about it."

"I can see that. She can be free to do what needs

to be done. Do you suppose she uses it a great deal around the house with the kids? Do they have any magic?" He told him how Trevor could see Finny. "That's good, right? Are there any other ghosts he can see?"

Finny lived in the house before Shawn moved in, and he was a hundred-year-old ghost. He could do some magic on his own, but it would wear him out, and he'd have to rest—which meant that you couldn't see him.

"Not that we've encountered. But I don't know that there are that many ghosts around the house anymore. They pretty much cleared out when Finny moved into the house. There are some at the graveyard that's in the back, but they don't bother us, and we don't interact with them." They talked about other magic that Shawn had and when she used it. It was nice having someone in the house who could do some extensive magic, but she never hurt anyone with it. He didn't even know if she could. "What's Taylor doing since she's not working for the foundation anymore? I heard that she was working on some projects for the kids this summer."

"She has a brilliant mind about things that the kids can do in the yard. I love it when she gets all crafty. She said that it's not crafting so much as it's an outlet for her mind and to get rid of some of the clutter that is around the house all the time." Jack laughed. "We'd not have any clutter if she didn't pick it up when she's out. But by the time summer is over, the kids have done some fun projects and have learned something. Are your kids going to join ours again this year?"

"I plan on it. Shawn said it gives her two whole hours once a month to just chill. I get to hang crafts all over my office for people to marvel at." Jack said that he has a refrigerator full of projects already that Taylor had made as trial pieces. "I bet that's fun too. The kids have fun, and that's all that matters to me. I bet that Taylor enjoys it more than the kids do. She sure looks like it at the end of one of her crafting days."

"She said that had she had it in her mind about having kids when she'd been younger, she might well have been a teacher. I don't see her enjoying that too much. They'd require her to teach something once in a while about the curriculum, and she just wants to have fun. Not to mention she'd have them outside every day. She does her best work in the yard where she has no restrictions." Ethan said he'd known that about her. "She's a free spirit, and I wouldn't have it any other way."

They talked about their wives while Ethan finished his meal. He didn't usually eat in the cafeteria when he was hungry because he'd get questions asked of him about how surgeries were going. The only thing he could do was refer them to the board that was on the wall that said where certain patients were at during some point in their surgery. And unless they had the number that went with their family member, he couldn't help them at all. Most people around town knew that he was head of surgery, and that's why they asked him about their loved ones.

After Jack left, he went back to his office and worked on the paperwork that was forever piling up. No matter how much he got done before lunch, there would be a stack of them on his desk when he got back. Today was no different. As he was sorting through files, he kept thinking about this morning and Mrs. Challenger. So far today, he'd been able to avoid her, but he wasn't going to be able to do that daily. They would meet at some point in the halls, and he didn't know what to say to her.

~*~

Jack had all the giveaways in the storage locker so that they'd not be out where people could get to them. Some of the things that businesses were donating to the dinner were valuable, and he didn't want to have to replace them if someone got into them. He closed and locked the door after putting the donation from the hospital—five sets of scrubs of any kind, plus five days off with pay for the person who won it. He thought that the scrubs sets alone would be worth the ticket, but he didn't know. He didn't have to buy them and wouldn't know the first thing about how much they cost.

"What did the Banquet Room donate? Last year, their gift was sort of lame. I don't think that many people put on it that they wanted it. Do you remember what it had been?" He told Taylor that it had been four place settings of dinnerware of their choice. "Yes, that's sort of lame. Did they do any better this year?"

"I don't know that I'd call it better, but it was something larger. This year they're giving away ten place settings and a dinner for two at the Banquet Room. I'm not sure how that will work for them. Do they usually have dinners for people coming in off the street?" Taylor told him that once a month, they do have that. "Then that might be good too. I don't know. I don't think I've ever eaten there."

"You haven't. Not with me anyway." She kissed him on the mouth, and he asked her what that was for. "For being you. I love you very much."

"You're off again, I take it?" She said that she wanted to hit the craft store as they were having a sale on glitter. "I know how you love glitter."

"It's the magical dust of summer. And it's going to be on every project that they make this summer. I know how Dever loves it." He really didn't. He called it something that he couldn't remember right now, but it wasn't nice. He only said it around the adults. "I'll be back before dinner. Is there anything that you'd like to have? It's cook's night off, and it'll just be the seven of us tonight. Trevor said something about making your own pizza, but I'd have to stop at the store if that's what you want."

"It is. It sounds fun too." Trevor usually would pick make your own something when the cook was off. Last week, it had been sundaes. It turned out to be really good, but the mess was something that he didn't like cleaning up afterwards. But the kids had fun, and he couldn't begrudge them something when they enjoyed it so much. "I can go to the store for the stuff we'll need. I don't mind at all."

"All right, but don't overdo it. Last time you got too much, and it was a week before we were able to get all the cheeses eaten. I love cheese too, but there was just too much of it." He knew that he'd get too much again and didn't mind the scolding.

As soon as he was ready to lock up the rest of the business, he headed home. He had to order some supplies for the next catering job, and he loved that he could save them so much money by ordering in bulk. The large walk-in freezer had saved them a lot of money since they put it in, and he was happy with the results. As soon as he was sitting at his desk, he heard from Denver.

"I have two things that I need to talk to you about. One of them isn't important, but it's just a question that I had. The other is something that I've been thinking about for a while now." He told him that he had time now to listen to him. *"Can I come over? It's something else I've*

been thinking about. I miss you while you're so busy all the time."

"I always have time to be visited by my family." He said he'd be over in an hour and was able to finish up the order before he showed up. Just as he was finishing up putting the order into the computer, Denver sat down across from him and looked sort of dejected. He asked him what was wrong.

"Nothing. Like I said, I miss you. With you working with Dakota all the time, it's hard to get to see you. What have you been up to?" He told him about the party they were going to cater for the hospital and about how he'd just put in an order for the next three projects. But he could tell that he was only about half listening to him, and he said that he was going to have a baby on his own since Taylor was so busy with her projects. "That's good. I was wondering if you've given any thought to having dinner with the brothers more than once a week. I really miss you guys a great deal, and it would do me some good to have you guys around more often."

"What's really bothering you?" He said it was that he missed them. "Something else is going on, and I don't know what it is. You have to tell me before I beat the living shit out of you. Tell me what's going on."

"I feel like time is slipping away from me." He asked him what he meant. "I don't know. Since

Grannie and Grandda passed away, I've been feeling my mortality a great deal. I don't regret having Parker take away my immortality, but I do miss you guys and would like to spend more time with you."

"You'd have to be more upbeat than you are right now." He said that he'd been feeling his death coming on. "What are you talking about? You have a lot of years left in your life. You have a great family and a home that you love. I don't understand where this is coming from."

"I don't either." He wiped his hand over his face and looked at him. He could see tears in his eyes, and he felt bad for his brother. Asking him again what was going on, he finally got up and started pacing the room. "Everything is just too perfect. Like you said, I have a great family that I love. A good job with being leap leader and I love my wife so much that I can't express in words how much I love her. But I'm waiting for the other shoe to drop, and everything will be gone."

"If Grannie were here, she would pop you in the back of your head. You have to stop waiting for things to go bad all the time." He said he knew that in his head, but his heart was elsewhere. "Well, get them on the same page. You're going to make yourself ill if you keep thinking—you've always been this way. How am I just now noticing it?"

"I don't know. Maybe I hide it well?" He told him that he wasn't hiding anything from him. "I know.

That's the reason I came to talk to you. I wanted to talk to someone who would tell me like it is. And I'm not disappointed in you right now. You've always been the one person that I could talk to."

"What about Bailee? Does she know how you're feeling?" He said that she had popped him in the head. "Good for her. I knew that I loved her a great deal."

"I'm making myself sick over this. I know that on some level, things are going to continue to go right, but right now, all I can think about is doom and gloom. I don't want to feel that way." He told him he needed to go home and hug his kids. "That does help a great deal. I can't believe how lucky I am to have such a wonderful family. And to have Bailee in my life is just like ice cream with cake."

"I tell you what. I'll get with the others, and we'll have a pity party for you." He told him he wasn't nice. "I wasn't planning to be. You need us to kick you in the ass, and we both know that they'll be all for it. I don't know what's wrong with you, but you're going to have to snap out of it before you make yourself ill. I've said this before, but you have a good life and everything a man could want in the world. Stop waiting for something bad to happen."

"I agree with you." He finally sat down and looked at him. "When did you become so smart? Is that something that I've missed?"

"Everyone misses how smart I am. Even Taylor

forgets sometimes when I'm around her." He laughed, which is what he'd been planning. "If nothing else, the two of us will have dinner more often. I'm betting that I can convince the others to join us. They love getting together as much as we do. And they won't allow you to be in self-pity mode for long."

"I already feel better. I wish I could be as free as the rest of you are from worrying." He told his brother that he worried all the time. "You don't show it. I need to be more like you are, rolling with the punches."

"I don't always feel like I'm going to lose everything, but when it hits me that I could, I go and hug my wife and children. They're the best medicine for any kind of bad thoughts." Denver said he'd have to do that more. "Good. You need to get your head out of your ass and remember that we are all doing well and that we're going to be doing this well in the future. Longevity is in our jeans, and we couldn't have a better role model on that than our grandparents. They lived to be a hundred years old. That gives you more than enough time to be more productive with your feelings."

"I know. I know. I just have to figure out a way to stay more positive. I'm going to take your advice and hug my family more, including my brothers. I miss that Margo and Grayson have moved away. They were so much like Grannie together that you sometimes forget that she's not her." He laughed and told him not to tell her that next time he saw her. "I won't. She'll bop me in the back of the head with something hard. I know she's got a bit of a mean streak inside of her."

He was glad to hear his brother laughing. He did worry about him and wondered what he was going to do to keep him upbeat. He wondered if having dinner with the family was going to be enough and decided that it would have to be. Letting the others know what was wrong with him might bring them all together more. It couldn't hurt, and he'd love to have dinner with his brothers more often.

After Denver left, looking better than he had when he showed up, he got back to work. Getting things set up for the following week always made him feel better, and when he realized that they had the weekend off starting on Friday, he thought that it would be the perfect time for them all to get together at his home. He called Taylor to see what she thought of his idea.

"I was just thinking about getting us all together yesterday. It's been a couple of weeks since we've had dinner together, and it will be fun." He agreed with her and told her that they'd just have things grilled out on the grill that way there wouldn't be too much in the way of cooking. "You'll have to pick up somethings for that as well. Maybe we can have someone cater it so that we don't have to worry about the clean-up either."

"Better idea all around." He marked his calendar

for the dinner and reached out to all of them to let them know. Maybe Margo and Grayson would make it, and that would be epic. Since they moved away, they'd not gotten to see each other very often.

Margo had started her own school, and it was a great success. He was so proud of the two of them that sometimes he'd think they had the best life of all of them. Only having the one child, they were the busiest family that he knew. Grayson was still working as a CEO of the foundation; he did it from afar, coming in once a week to make sure that things were going the way that they should be. So far, he'd not had any problems with the foundation, and he thought that it should make Denver happy. He was going to talk to his wife about his brother at dinner tonight. They had to get him on the right page with life, or he really was going to get himself sick.

Picking up the things they'd need for dinner tonight, he was happy that Taylor was going to be ordering the food for the catering service. He loved that they could afford to have it done that way. He got to spend more time with his family without having to worry about the clean-up, and could visit more. He thought that being with his family was the best balm that he'd ever had. When he got home, the kids were ready to eat, so he started portioning out things that they'd want on their pizzas before Taylor came home.

With a kiss to her mouth, he decided that he had

the best wife of all his family. She was so free-spirited that he found himself laughing with her about the strangest things. She, of course, had to show him what she'd been able to pick up at the store, and he loved that she'd been able to get everything on sale. She was a bargain hunter if nothing else.

Chapter 10

Colby looked over the schedules that he had on the wall and thought that everything looked like it was working out. He had a fleet of ten ships now and couldn't believe that he employed over a hundred people. The deep-sea fishing was going well, and he was still having fun.

While he didn't go out on the trips as much as he did when he first started out, he was still getting them ready to go. Just yesterday, he'd been able to pick up a short run, and he'd forgotten how much he'd enjoyed it. As soon as they docked, the fishermen, catching their limit in the few hours they'd been out, were singing his praises and wanting to book a three-day adventure for next month. He handed them the contract and the flyer that Shawn had made for him, and was happy that they were so happy. He smiled when he was able to see what he'd been missing and wondered if he should do it more often.

He might just do that to keep his mind on what went on when they were out on the sea and fishing. He'd been lax in going out, and he couldn't think of a single reason that he hadn't been doing it more often. Other than the fact that he was so busy with his family that he really didn't have the time.

He and Emma had four children, all boys but for the one girl. He loved coming home to them when he'd been busy all day and couldn't believe how much fun he was having with being a dad. As soon as he got home, he gathered them up together and did homework. It wasn't much, but he would keep on top of it just for them. He wanted them to be successful and hoped that it showed in the way that he ran his business. Emma came home about an hour after he'd been home, and he told her that he loved her.

"I love you too. I've had a good day today and couldn't wait to share it with you. But now all I can think about is getting together with your family on Friday and having fun. You did know about it, right?" He said that Jack had contacted him. "Good. It's been a couple of months since we've been together. Jack even said that he thought Margo and Grayson would be there. I hope so. I miss them both so much."

"I do too. But I'm happy for the two of them, too." She said that she was proud of them for having started their own business. "If anyone could run a school, it would be her. She is so organized that it used to boggle my mind how well she could put things together. And she helped me study for tests, too, by showing me how to map things out."

"I've seen her scheduling, and I have to admit that I was jealous. You should see her Christmas schedule. She has things planned out for the minute." The two of them laughed as they gathered the kids up for dinner. They were having pasta for their meal tonight, and it was one of their kids' favorite meals. "I might have to go out later tomorrow. There are three applicants on the desk that need to be looked over. I didn't think about it being Thursday and the weekend coming up, so I have to go and make sure that someone goes over them. They're for a couple of families that are down on their luck. I love helping families that need help. It makes me feel like this is just what the foundation is about."

"I saw some kids on the dock today. They were begging for work. I had them help the clients get their catch together and take them to the cars. I paid them in cash, hoping that it would help them. I have a feeling that they're going to be coming around a bunch now. I don't mind until they become too much. Understand?" She said that she did as she cut the lasagna into squares for the kids. "I love you so very much."

"I love you as well." Then the kids started saying how much they loved the two of them, and it made him laugh. He loved his family so much that he felt like he was the luckiest man alive. "We love you guys as well, so eat your dinner."

It was messy having pasta with the kids. They would eat it well, but they still got sauce all over themselves and each other. When it was time for dessert, the kids only wanted a dish of ice cream, while he and Emma skipped it. He didn't care for sweets all that much, so he didn't mind when he didn't have any. Emma said that she'd have some fruit later, and he knew that she would. She did love apples and kiwi together, and he'd have a bit for himself.

After bathing the kids and getting them into their beds, he sat on the couch with Emma, and they talked about their day. Like her, he was excited about having dinner with the family on Friday and couldn't wait to see them all together. The kids would be a great distraction, but they would play with their cousins all evening and be ready for bed when dinner was over. He wondered if, like the last time dinner had been catered, if they'd have a different meal for the kids. They would eat hot dogs over steak, and he thought all the kids were like that.

"I'm thinking that Kayce and Molly will be having their baby soon. How many will that make them?" He told her it was six. "Of course, they'd have the most kids, with him being the youngest."

"He's the best at bandaging them up, too. Did you hear about the babysitter that they hired so that they could go to dinner? She left the kids there by themselves because her boyfriend called her. I would have murdered her. To leave my kids like that? Well, they'd never find her body again." He laughed, hoping that she was joking. His wife could be furious when it came to their kids. All of them. "She even expected them to pay her for the whole night, too. I guess Kayce called her mom and got her into trouble. She's not supposed to see the boyfriend when she's supposed to be working."

"His kids are good kids, too. Which one of them called their parents? I know it was one of them who did it. They're very protective of their siblings, too." She told him it was Carrie, the oldest. "She's scary smart, isn't she? I was talking to her the other day, and I couldn't believe that she's only twelve. I thought for sure I was talking to an adult. She claims that she's going to be the king of our kind someday. After she takes Denver's job of pride leader."

"I would believe it." They relaxed on the couch, and he laughed a little. "What? Did you think of something that I'm going to think is funny too? I could always use a good laugh."

"I was thinking of what Ronin would say if he knew she was gunning for his job. He'd probably be impressed that she thought she could at such a young age. She's the oldest twelve-year-old that I know, and that's saying a lot. I have about half a dozen twelve-year-old nieces and nephews around now."

"I guess she's taking college classes online. I don't envy her parents having someone that smart around all the time." He agreed with his Emma and told her that he was glad that his kids were just above average. "That's not right either. I think our kids are brilliant."

They talked about their kids for a while and got a laugh out of how much they were into things. They did talk about Taylor having them over in the summer months and wondered how she did it. He knew that while he looked forward to having them gone to her house, they didn't want to have to clean up after they were gone.

"There is so much glitter." Emma told him how Taylor was going to make sure that everything had glitter on it this year, as she found out that Denver hated it. "He does. He said that months from now, he'd find it on something in a room that no glitter had been in before. He said that his car sparkles all the time from when he picked them up from the house. I bet she does just that and makes sure that it's all over everything."

When they were headed up to bed, he locked up the house. He did it nightly and was glad that his family was safe. As soon as he was on the stairs to go up to their room, Carter, their second-oldest son, said that he wanted something more to eat. Not one to turn them down when they were hungry, he took him to the kitchen to find that sandwiches had been made for them, and he shared one with him. As he sat there eating his part of the sandwich, he looked up at him.

"How do you know when you find your mate?" He told him what he'd been able to do when he found his mom. "I thought so. I think that I found her. My mate, I mean."

He didn't know what to say when he said that, so he waited for him to say more. To find one's mate so young was rare, but it did happen. He asked him who it was. Not sure who Connie Gibbons was, he asked where he'd seen her before.

"She's in my class. She said that I'm not to touch her. And I don't. She can be really intense when she has something to say, Dad." He barely caught his laugh. This was too serious for him to think that something was funny. "She smells like a girl, no problem, but when I'm around her, I want to protect her something terrible. She can take care of herself, so I just make sure that she's not going to be hurt. And I can change my clothes when I get out of the shower. I think that one told me the most."

"Yes, that's the one that got me." He sat down on the chair and waited for his son to say more. When he didn't, he asked him if he was sure. "I mean, she could just be a girl that happens to be nice to you."

"Oh no, she's not nice to me at all. She's kind of mean all the time." He did laugh then, and his son looked at him oddly. "I know that sometimes mates can be bossy, but I'm not sure what to do with her. I think I'm going to let her protect me when I need it."

"Good thinking." He played with a second sandwich before taking a bite out of it. "Have you told her yet? I mean, does she know—is she a lion?"

"She's a lion, but darker than mine. I can tell by her hair color. She's going to be a beautiful cat when she can shift. And no, I didn't tell her anything, but she told me. I guess she can change her clothing, too. Are you mad at me, Dad?" He asked him why he'd be mad at him for finding his other half. "Because I'm only ten years old. I didn't mean for it to happen."

"Of course you didn't. But you're lucky. You know who you're going to be spending the rest of your life together with, and that's a good thing." He nodded, still unsure looking. "As you grow older, you'll learn to appreciate her and her moods. I hope so anyway. You two will get to grow old together, too. That's a good thing."

"I guess so. I just didn't know how you were going to take me finding my mate. I've wanted to tell you for the last few days." He had to wonder how much he'd been going through with his thoughts of having a mate when he was so young. But he knew that he had a good head on his shoulders and that he knew the rules of having a mate. "I won't ever force her into anything that she doesn't want to do. I know that's important. But I'm scared to meet her daddy. He's been at school picking her up, and he gives me the evil eye. I'm staying away from him."

"If he gives you any trouble, you come to me or your mom." He asked if he'd tell her. "I will as soon as possible. But if Mr. Gibbons says one thing to you that makes you feel bad, you tell me, and I'll have a talk with him."

"Don't kill him." He promised that he wouldn't. He just hoped that he'd be able to keep that promise. "I don't want to have to visit you in prison. I want you to be there when we get married. I know that's a long way off, but you might get life or something like that and not get out in time to be there for me."

After having a bit more of a conversation about being mates, his son said he was tired. Taking him up to bed, he tucked him into the covers and told him again how proud he was of him. While he was very worried, he knew that his son hadn't had anything to do with finding his mate. It was just something that happened, and he was going to be happy for him.

Telling Emma about what they talked about, he found that he had about a million more questions than he had answers for. When she asked what they were to do, Colby said there was nothing they could do but to keep an eye on things. She asked if he thought that Mr. Gibbons was going to be a problem.

"He'll only be a problem once." She shivered when he said that, and he pulled her into his arms. "I'll talk to Denver about it. He might have more information on childhood mates than anyone would. At times like these, I wish my grannie and grandda were around. They'd know just what to do and what to do about Gibbons. He'd better not hurt our son, or he'll be in a world of hurt himself."

"I agree on both accounts. Telling your brother will get you information on Gibbons, too. He might even have some ideas on what to do about how this will affect them both as they get older. Have you ever heard of something like this happening?" He told her that he'd heard about it but never knew anyone that it had happened to. "We'll just hope that Denver or even Ronin will have some advice. I'm really proud of him for telling you. I thought that something was bothering him, but I didn't know how serious it was. I'm glad you told me."

"He wanted me to tell you. I think he wants me to talk to Denver, too. To maybe tell him what he's to do." She asked if there was much he could do. "No. Not now, at any rate. He'll just know that she's his mate for all time, and they'll be happy. Hopefully."

"That's what I'm going to be thinking from now on. At least we know that he's found his other half and he's going to be happy." Turning off the light on his side of the bed, he snuggled with Emma. "I'm not going to say anything to him unless he brings it up. That way I don't embarrass him."

He didn't think she would, but it might be a good idea to wait for him to speak first. As he was closing his eyes to sleep, he thought of all the things that would go right for the two of them. They'd grow up together, and that would be a good thing for all of them.

~*~

Kayce heard about his nephew and wondered how he was doing. Something like this happening could be traumatic to someone as young as he was, but he wasn't too worried. The kid had a good head on his shoulders and had talked to Denver. It was the way that he'd go if it were to happen to one of his kids."

Dinner was to be served in forty-five minutes, and he was starving. He'd been looking forward to this meal all day, and now it was about time to eat. All he could think about was that he was glad that they'd been able to get together. He loved his family.

"You look good, little brother. The tan looks good on you." He told Margo that he missed her. After getting a hug and a kiss from her, they sat down at one of the many tables. "And I missed all of you as well. I can't believe that it's been three months since we've all been together. It seems like it's been longer."

"I know what you mean." He heard one of the kids screaming and looked around for the one who had been hurt. It must not have been too much, as he wasn't bombarded with kids telling him he needed his case. "I go through more band aids when we all get together than I use at my practice. I actually buy them by the gross."

"That's a lot of knees to bandage up." They both

laughed, and he asked her how she was doing. "I didn't realize how much I needed this dinner until I showed up here. I've really missed everyone so much."

"I know that I've missed you, too. But we all understand why you had to move so far away. It's been so nice that you have your own school, but it's not the same with you not being around all the time. How is Grayson doing? I missed him the last time he was in for a meeting." She said that he was doing great, having fun being in charge of the foundations. "I knew that if anyone could do that job, it would be him. He's always been good with numbers and such. I guess he's been wanting to expand, too. I hope he finds someone to do that for us. It'll be nice to spread what we have to someone else."

"That's what he said. And the Fosters are happy with it as well. They said that the foundation money would go towards the next charity and so on after that. I guess they'll help out, but won't be as much of a part of it as they were with us. I think they're going to be passing it on to us to make it work." He asked her if she thought that they could. "Yes. We've made a success of it, and it's helped so many people. I would love to see it go on. Wouldn't you?"

"Yes." He thought about asking her if she'd be a part of it and realized that she was. She would give up time with Grayson when he was around here working. And when he worked from home. "I never thought about how much time we've given to the foundation. Not just working the phone when we first started out, but even getting our family to work the shifts that are needed to keep it running. I might not be there as much as I should, but when I work, I devote my entire time to it."

"That's the way it should be. And the next family will hopefully be able to do it like we have. Moving our entire family out here at once was a huge undertaking. It worked out, but I do wonder how much harder it will be on the next group or family." He said that he didn't know, but was hopeful like she was. "I'm hoping it's a large family that does it rather than a group of people. As a family we pulled together to get things going. As a group of people, you never know what it's going to be like. Maybe I'm thinking too hard on this."

"No, I think you're right. We only had each other, and that was enough for us at the time." He thought about how much time they still devoted to the charity and was happy that he was able to say no when it became too much for him. "I still have nightmares about the first day we opened, and Denver was hurt. All that blood. Even being a doctor, I sort of froze up because I knew who it was."

"I think about that every once in a while and have the same thoughts. I was there that day, and the man was going to blow up the entire building with all of us in it." She grabbed his hand and held it. "I love you, Kayce. I don't want anything to happen to any of you."

"I don't either." They talked about the next charity foundation, and he was glad that he wasn't going to be that big a part of it. Mostly, it would be Grayson and Denver as they were the only two full-time people who worked it from the family. He'd be asked to train some people, and he was all right with that. But he didn't want to get involved like he had when they first opened their doors. "I was thinking that this is going to be a lot of work for Grayson. Will you guys be able to be apart for that long? I know that after a few hours without Molly, I'm really missing her."

"We've gotten used to being able to go for a couple of days without each other. I'm not saying it'll be easy; it won't be. But we have a strong marriage and are great at pulling the weight of the other person when they're not around. It also helps that we only have one child. You and Molly must have your hands full with six and one on the way. She looks ready to pop."

"She said she feels that way sometimes." He looked across the yard at his mate and love of his life. She was currently holding one of their other children and talking to Grayson. "She only has about six weeks to go, then we'll have our child. I've never been so happy to be a dad when they all gather around me. It's like my own slice of heaven."

"I know what you mean. I might only have the one, but it's great when she's around. I feel complete." He told her that was exactly how he felt. "Good. If you get any more complete, you're going to have to get a bigger house."

"We were actually talking about adding onto our home. It wouldn't be that hard. And I think before we're finished, we're going to need the extra room. I don't know how many kids she wants, but I'm happy to help her along with that. The more the merrier, she tells me all the time." She laughed so hard that people turned and looked at her. "Only you would think that's funny. Most people would admonish me for saying something about sex. Not you."

"I know how babies are made." She leaned back in her seat and looked around. "Do you ever regret coming out here? I don't mean about you not meeting Molly, but I'm talking about the move. It was so much. And I don't think that without the help of the Fosters we could have made it in one piece."

"Sometimes I think about what we left behind. The friends that we had. The house that we all grew up in. I wonder at times if it's still standing and if a big family is enjoying the foundation that the house gave us. But then I think about meeting Molly and being so close to all my family, and I think it was well worth it. I doubt very much I would have had my own practice if we'd have stayed there." She nodded as if she understood. "I do like the weather out here better. It's wonderfully cool year-round."

"I met Grayson at the other house, so it holds a bit more for us than it would for you. I loved the old house, too, and miss being able to call it home. The house that we had when we first moved here was all right, but the home we have now is so much more. We got to pick it out for ourselves, and I've learned that makes a huge difference in how you feel about a place. Don't get me wrong, I loved the other place, but where we are now means so much to us that it's doubtful if we ever move again." He told her that was the way they felt about their home. "You did so much to the house to make it your own. It must have cost you a fortune to have all the rooms done the way that they are."

"We had a little help from Molly's grannie." He told her about finding the money in the walls and the letter from her grannie. How she'd won the lottery so many times that she'd been able to put away all the cash from it so that Molly would have something to work with when it came to upgrading the house. "Well, aren't you lucky. You never told me this before."

"You're the first person that I've told in all these years of finding it. Don't say anything, please? I don't want anyone coming back on us to take it from us." She asked if Molly's brothers were still alive. "They all three are. Her dad, William, ended up getting four life sentences for his part in three murders. Not to mention his involvement in the Social Security scams he had going on. Both of her brothers got life each without any chance of parole. But you never know with the court systems if someone will actually stay in prison or not, just because they have life sentences."

"No, you don't." He thanked her for being there for him. "We always were close, the two of us. I hoped that it had to do with the fact that I was so much older than you are, but I don't know anymore. I'm enjoying just hanging out with you."

Dinner was called, and Margo ended up sitting next to him and Molly. Grayson was still talking and missed his chance to sit next to his mate. Oh well, Grayson could make friends anywhere, and with this family, he was always able to hold his own in a conversation. Before they were set to eat, Denver called them all to order by gently hitting his fork next to his glass. He cleared his throat and was told to get on with it; they were hungry. Everyone laughed.

"It's been nearly fifteen years since we moved here fresh out of our home state. I wanted to say that it's been wonderful being here with all of you and how much I appreciate all the time you've given to the foundation." There was applause, and someone said it was all because of him. "I would like to take credit for that, but we all know that it wouldn't have been possible without the two people that we've lost. Grannie and Grandda. If they had not been on board and as supportive as they had been, none of us would be here today." Another round of applause, and Denver started to sit down, but stood up again. "I almost forgot something. The next foundation is going to be called the LouCinda and Hudson Charitable Foundation. After the two greatest people I've ever known."

People patted him on the back when he sat down the second time, and he wanted to hug his brother for what was going to be done for their grandparents. As soon as dinner was being set on the table, he got up and hugged his brother tightly. Crying a little, the two of them held onto each other like they hadn't seen each other in a while. When it had only been an hour since they were talking about the meal.

Kayce did end up bandaging a couple of knees and one cheek. The kids were roughhousing but having fun as kids did. Once he told them that they were going to live to fight another day, he sat back down but kept his bag close. He knew that his brother Ethan had his around as well—just in case.

When dinner was over, and the kids were playing in the large pool, he continued to sit with Margo and enjoyed himself. They had been close all their lives, and she was the one who had bandaged his knees when Grannie hadn't been around to do it.

Just as he was thinking it was time to get his

own kids home and into bed, he thought that he saw ghostly figures. No one else seemed to see the two of them, but he knew it was his grandparents. Then he saw that Shawn was looking in the same direction. She turned and looked around and spotted him looking at them too. Raising her glass up, she tilted it in his direction, and he felt his heart expand with love. They were there, and he had to wonder if they had been to every meeting of the family when they got together and saw no reason to believe that they'd not be there. Wanting to go to them and touch them somehow, he watched as they faded away. Just as it should have been, they made sure that they were all right before moving on. He would treasure this memory forever and knew that he'd been given a special gift.

"Did you see them?" Instead of answering his brother, he hugged them. "I can't believe after all this time they showed up to see us. And on a night when we're all together." He'd forgotten that Ethan could see ghosts, too, and hugged him again. "I've never seen them before at other gatherings. It was special that they were here for this one, and they showed up. I'm so happy I could bust."

After getting his kids home, he told Molly what he'd been able to see. She cried when he told her they looked just like they did when they'd been alive, and she hugged him tightly. Molly had only gotten to spend a few years with them, but she said that she made every moment count.

Going to bed himself that night, he thought about all the years that he'd been living here. All the things that he'd seen had changed with the years. After holding Molly for a few minutes, he got up and went to each of his children's rooms and hugged them gently. He was a happy man, and nothing in this world could take that away from him.

Before You Go...

HELP AN AUTHOR

write a review

THANK YOU!

Share your voice and help guide other readers to these wonderful books. Even if it's only a line or two, your reviews help readers discover the author's books so they can continue creating stories that you'll love. Log in to your favorite retailer and leave a review. Thank you.

Kathi S. Barton is an award-winning and bestselling author known for her steamy paranormal romances and unforgettable characters. A recipient of the prestigious Pinnacle Book Achievement Award, her books have topped the charts on Amazon and All Romance eBooks, earning her a loyal global readership.

Kathi lives in Nashport, Ohio, with her husband, Paul. When she's not crafting passionate love stories set in magical worlds, she enjoys camping, exploring local auctions, and attending county fairs, where Paul showcases his artwork and pottery. Her creative spark—fueled by a muse she describes as a cross between Jimmy Stewart and Hugh Jackman—brings her stories to vivid, heartfelt life.

Paranormal romance with plenty of heat is her favorite genre, and she loves connecting with her readers. Feel free to reach out—Kathi would love to hear from you.

www.ingramcontent.com/pod-product-compliance
Lightning Source LLC
LaVergne TN
LVHW090516110826
845146LV00003B/877

* 9 7 9 8 8 9 1 2 6 5 2 2 6 *